MW01059211

Blood Knot

Books by Pete Fromm

The Tall Uncut

Indian Creek Chronicles

King of the Mountain

Monkey Tag

Dry Rain

Blood Knot

Blood Knot

Stories by Pete Fromm

THE LYONS PRESS

Printed in the United States of America

10 9 8 7 6 5 4 3 2 1

Design by John Gray

Library of Congress Cataloging-in-Publication Data
Fromm, Pete, 1958–
    Blood knot / Pete Fromm.
        p.   cm.
    Contents: Blood knot—The net—Home before dark—Natives,
boxcars, and transplants—Trying to be normal—Stone—Grayfish—My
sister's hood—For the kid's sake—Mighty mouse and blue cheese from
the moon.
    ISBN 1-55821-744-4
    1. United States—Social life and customs—20th century—Fiction.
2. Married people—United States—Fiction. 3. Family—United
States—Fiction. 4. Domestic fiction, American. 5. Fishing stories,
American.   I. Title.
PS3556.R5842B58   1998
813'.54—dc21   98-6485
                                                              CIP

For MARTIN K. MEYER,

who first showed me the ways of the fly line,

and years later led me to his own Grandpa's Creek

Contents

Acknowledgments

I am grateful to the following publications in which these stories originally appeared: *Fly Rod & Reel:* "Blood Knot" and "Home Before Dark" as the winner of the first Robert Traver Fiction Award. *Big Sky Journal:* "Natives, Boxcars, and Transplants." *American Way:* "Trying to Be Normal" (in much different form as "Paddlefish"). *Montana Crossroads:* "Trying to be Normal" (in its present form). *Gray's Sporting Journal:* "Stone," "Grayfish," and "Mighty Mouse and Blue Cheese from the Moon."

"Home Before Dark" and "Grayfish" also appeared in the collection *King of the Mountain,* 1994, Stackpole Books.

"Mighty Mouse and Blue Cheese from the Moon" also appeared in the collection *The Tall Uncut,* 1998, the Lyons Press.

Blood Knot

The money's not as thick as it could be. No great clots of it lying about, tripping anybody up, if you know what I mean. One disaster after another. You know the drill. So the plans I'd made in court (had shoved up my backside, really) looked like something from another planet. Reading over the custody stuff, what you have to wonder, after the usual *Is this really in English?* is *Were they even talking about me?*

But my name's there at the top. So's Carly's. And Kenny's. The child in contention.

Right there in black and white, even if it is in Mandarin or whatever, it says that the expense of all visitation is the sole responsibility of The Father. I.e. (as they would say), if I get to see Kenny, it's out of my pocket. Pockets that at the time had me talking about airfares and excursions to Disney World, because, of course, the first thing Carly insists on is moving back to Georgia. Like that's a place to raise anything but a peanut.

Airfare's out of the question now, of course. Greyhound's out of the question, for crying out loud. Even before the child-support garnishment.

But I can't just not see Kenny. Can't let her haul him out there to cut me off. Can't bear the idea of seeing him all grown up some day, bowling me over with some southern gentleman's drawl.

So I drive it, like that's really any less expensive than anything else. But time is all I've got now that's cheap, so I log the hours and the miles, missing work, wearing out the truck. Montana, Wyoming, Colorado, Kansas, Missouri, Arkansas, Tennessee (for a few minutes), Mississippi, Alabama, and finally Georgia. Places I'd never been; stretches in there that'd bore a monk to suicide.

When at last I follow the directions down the final pleasant blocks to Carly's new home, I'm a little worse for wear. Slept in rest stops the whole way down, stretched out in back. Skipped sleeping altogether the last night, too excited to see him again, pushing straight through. Haven't changed my clothes or showered in three days, I realize, and I'm just about to screech out, find some truck stop somewhere where I can clean up, when Kenny comes bursting through Carly's new screen door, like he's been waiting since the day she took him away.

It takes me a second to get my trembling fingers to open the damn seat belt and, I tell you, I about break down right there. Ears whining with road roar, back all stove up with the miles, I lurch out onto the street, the hot, wet air laying me low, so different than anything I'm used to. Kenny rounds the front of the truck and I drop to my knees and scoop him up, tears rolling down my face that I rub off in his hair before he gets a chance to see.

Carly waits on the porch, arms folded across her chest, barely allowing Kenny to give me a tour of the place, his new room, new toys, everything he's chattering about. Too soon we're back out front with Carly, no cup of coffee, no "How was the ride?" no "How've you been?" No anything. Just her standing there not quite looking at me, like I'm something particularly nasty the tide's washed in.

So I touch Kenny's head and ask, "What's the scoop, boyo? What do you have planned for us?" knowing it should've been me doing the planning, that I should have had everything arranged, instead of worrying just about getting here.

But Kenny grins. "Let's go home," he says right away, meaning Montana, any distance less than nothing to him. "Let's fish the Dearborn. You've still got our raft, right? And we can walk up the Sun. We can even . . ."

I hold up a hand. "We're not getting anywhere just standing here." I glance at Carly, truer words never spoken. "Grab your bag and throw it in the truck."

But instead of flying at the offer like he always has, Kenny hesitates, watching his mom and me squared off, closer than he's seen us in months and months. So I cry, "They're getting away!" our old fishing call, and he finally jumps.

Kenny's "Let's go home" is the victory I hold when Carly barely waits for the door to bang shut behind him before demanding to know, "You're going to drive him to Montana and back?"

"He said that's what he wants. What'd you have in mind? A trip to the zoo?"

"How long did it take you to get here?"

"Long enough," I answer, turning to actually face her. "I suppose you couldn't have taken him any farther without putting your house up on stilts."

"Forty-eight hours of driving?"

"Thirty-eight."

"How much did you sleep?"

"I slept plenty. Don't start worrying about me now."

She gives me a look that lets me know exactly how concerned she is about me. "I won't let him go if you're just going to fall asleep at the wheel."

I stare at a point somewhere off her left shoulder.

"You have two weeks," she says. "Fourteen days."

She waits for me to answer.

"You'll spend half of it on the road, won't you? Just to spite me."

"Carly," I say, taking a slow, deep breath of the thick air. "If this could have less to do with you, I'd sure like to hear you explain how."

"It has everything to do with me!" she starts, hissing low as any snake. "I'm his mother!"

And then, thank God, Kenny's standing there, watching us, his duffel bag dragging down a shoulder. "They're getting away!" I say again, and he grins, running to throw his bag in the back of the truck.

"Two weeks," I say, and I can't stop myself from adding, "See how it feels." I walk away backward, so if Carly wants to shoot something else at me, it won't be in the back. But she just watches me go, only saying, "Don't you dare let anything happen to him."

I get the door shut behind me without slamming it and say, "Wave to your mom, Kenny," and that's how we pull out, Kenny waving, Carly standing like a ramrod, a smoking pillar of all our old anger, me reeking like I've been on the bum all my life.

"They're getting away," I whisper to myself.

4

◆ ◆ ◆

The skipped night, all the miles, have taken their toll, but having Kenny with me again keeps me going a long way. After hours of it, though, Kenny's babble about school, new friends, one actually named Blackwell, and another, no lie, called Rhett—a second grader who "Frankly, doesn't give a damn"—it all gets a little blurry. First time I've seen him in months, and to tell the truth, he's close to boring the pants off of me. Makes me feel like maybe Carly was right, that there is this gaping black hole where my heart's supposed to be.

I find myself strangling the wheel, fighting to keep the truck on the road, keep my eyes open, keep listening to Kenny's every word—now some hilarious story about his schoolteacher and the farting sound her chair makes—when we pop out of the maddening green tunnel of the old highway and swoosh onto a bridge. We're over water, a little river you couldn't have known was there fifty yards back. Nothing like Montana's sketchy cottonwood lines breaking the broad open of the valleys, advertising the rarity of water long before you can reach it.

We flash past a small, rusted sign naming the water: the Chattahoochee or Choctawhatchee. Whatsitwhosee. Something along those lines. Before I know what I'm doing I'm standing on the brakes, Kenny grabbing the dash, eyes wide, ready to laugh or scream or both. For crying out loud, I think, I haven't even made him buckle his seat belt.

Then we're stopped, the nose-curling stench of the tire's burned rubber eddying through the open windows. Kenny peeks at me. "What?"

"It's a long haul back home," I say, hoping my voice isn't shaking. "What say we give your new home waters a test?"

"Fish?" he asks. "Here?"

It makes me grin. At eight years old he knows water, has an eye for Montana streams, for where trout should rightly lie. I glance back in the rearview, but the river's already swallowed by the forest around the road. I remember just the flash of walnut brown water, roiled by some slow current. "Let's see what might be lurking in there."

"Some kind of bayou monster probably," he says.

I swing open my door, everything dead quiet without the roar of wind. I swear, you could swim through what they've got for air down here. Back home we've got bushes, brush—here it's vegetation; vegetation growing off of more vegetation. Looks like a Tarzan movie. Like living at the bottom of a salad bowl.

I start digging through the junk in the back of my truck, looking for the rods. "Bet there are catfish in there that could chew off your leg," I say. "Swallow you whole." The place gives me the creeps—wouldn't even be a surprise to see the Creature from the Black Lagoon come shuffling out of that mess—and I turn to see if I might actually be scaring Kenny.

But he's right there beside me, asking if I brought his rod, too, which of course I did, Carly having refused to take it with her. "There'll be other things for him to be interested in there," she'd said, Kenny already safely whisked off to her parents in Georgia. "At last," she'd added.

I hand Kenny the new case, warning him that it still holds the same old rod, not to get his hopes up. I just thought that rattling around in the back of the truck all this way, it might be best to keep it safe. "It'll be a while," I tell him, "before either of us waves around any new fishing gear." But I regret it immediately. The last thing he needs now is to be saddled with my finances. Or lack of same.

He's just glad to see his fishing rod again. He jabs the two pieces together, impatient for me to dig the reel out of my vest. "What should we try?" he asks, threading line through the eyelets.

"Not a clue," I admit. "I don't know what'll be in here, if it's anything that'll look at a fly."

I take a big Royal Wulff, something that'll be easy for him to see, and reach to tie it on for him.

But Kenny pulls his rod away, holds his hand out instead. "I can tie it on," he says. "I've been practicing."

With what? I want to ask, but hold my tongue, watching his own tongue poke from the corner of his mouth as he winds the leader around itself, trapping the eye of the hook.

"I got this string," he volunteers. "At night I tie it around the bedpost. Clinch knot, bowline, clove hitch. Or to itself: blood knot, fisherman's, sheep's bend."

I stare at him finishing his knot, biting off the free end. I clear my throat. "Why?" I ask.

"So I don't forget," he answers with a little roll of his eyes. "'You have to know your knots.'"

He's quoting me, knots, of all things, something I once thought could be important.

Walking to the bridge, we fight our way down to the river. The jungle hangs right over the edge. There's no place to even begin to cast and, with the water transparent as a plank, no telling what you could do to yourself wading. We stand and watch the water ooze by, our rods pointed over it, as if they were wands we could wave, simply dancing the fish out.

"Hmm," I say.

Kenny answers with his own "Hmmm."

"Not much the same as home, is it?" I ask.

He pushes at the wet tangle, worried about casting. "Hound Creek is like this some places."

I turn to him gaping. Hound Creek was half his life ago. "You remember that?"

"Right before the canyon. You said, 'Thick as the short hairs and twice as curly.'"

I blink and swallow.

He smiles. "I said that to Rhett, but he didn't know what I was talking about."

"That's good," I mumble. "That's probably not something you need to say. Definitely not around your mom."

He gives this exaggerated slap to his forehead, whispers, "Duh!"

And I crack up. We stand there laughing beside this impossible little stream in the place where he'll grow up now, laughing our heads off. I sit down on the one open spot and hold out my arms, and Kenny crawls into my lap and we keep laughing.

"There's got to be fish down here," I say at last, wiping at my eyes. "Some kind. Bass maybe. You'll learn what there is, how to fish it. Maybe with bait casters, big old crankbaits. Haul out some real hawgs."

Kenny curls his nose, and I'm embarrassed to see I've already instilled a fly fisherman's snobbery.

"You play what you're dealt, Kenny," I say, and with him still on my lap I take his hands in mine, his rod still held tight in his long, thin fingers.

"What if the whole game stinks?" he asks.

I can't answer. Instead I work out a little of his line, sidearm flips, his hands stiff under mine, working his Wulff upstream, letting it drift back the few feet right beneath the overhanging brush, dancing in the broken water of the shoreline.

"This is how you do it when it's tight like this," I explain. "If you can't wade out into the middle to weave your backcast over the creek's path."

"Wade in there?" he asks, his voice climbing in disbelief.

"That's what I mean."

"Catfish'd chew off your leg. Swallow you whole. Crawdads pick your bones."

We sit there together making our puny casts for longer than there's any fishing reason to, until finally Kenny says, "Dad, there's nothing that's going to eat that fly."

"I know," I whisper.

"Maybe we should get driving again."

I let go of his hands, leave his rod to him, and wrap my arms all the way around him, what we used to call gorilla hugs, beating our chests afterward. "Do you have any idea how far away Montana is?" I ask.

"I flew here, Dad. I saw the whole world down there. That's how far it is."

"That's about right," I say. And then, hating to, but admitting that this is our life now, I say, "Maybe, Kenny, maybe instead of hauling back down all those old roads, maybe we should give this place a try. See if we can't figure out how to fish around here. So you'll still be able to when I'm gone." I look out at the lazy curls churning the creek's dark surface. "So you won't have to tie knots around your bedpost."

"I can do most of them in the dark now," he answers. Then, so quiet I nearly don't hear, he adds, "After Mom turns off the light. When I'm supposed to be sleeping." He doesn't know how much to admit, I realize, how much parent I am anymore, how much partner.

"You're an expert," I say, pushing us both up to our feet. "I've never seen a better knot tyer than you. Ever."

◆ ◆ ◆

For three days we bumble around Alabama and Georgia, casting tiny trout flies onto tannin brown water as I lose all hope that anything of Kenny will survive this smothering, damp country. We sleep in the back of the truck, in any little pull-out we find, once in an interstate rest area after I nearly caved in to the temptation to haul him back north, take him on the lam, let Carly see if she can overcome her dread of that place long enough to come looking. As we travel along, the green thick enough to leave stains on us, the soaking heat wearing us down, the sleeping bags clammier and moldier every night, I see, for the first time, what Montana must have been to her; after the mountains were, like me, just something she saw every day. What a cold, hard, bone-dry place it must have been.

Once we ask a clump of black men hunkered over motionless poles what they're using. "Hell," I say, trying to smile, "we'll settle for just knowing what you're trying to catch."

Doughballs is the answer. For catfish. Kenny nearly retches on the spot.

Every night Kenny asks if he shouldn't call his mom. At first I tell him that she thinks we're on the road, halfway back to Montana, that she won't be expecting any calls. "We're footloose!" I bluster. "Can't let a phone anchor us down." But I can see that, one, Kenny's beginning to wish we *were* on the road back to Montana, and two, he doesn't really believe she isn't waiting for a call. The little pleasure I'd been taking at picturing her listening to my phone ring on and on, her disbelief that I'd disconnected the answering machine, her slamming her own phone back down on its hook, begins to wither.

At last, though I've always hated seeming like an outsider, some damn tourist, I stop in a bait shop and ask the old coots hanging around the counter if there's something more active than catfish working the local waters, if there's any place a guy could fly fish around here.

The shop is even swampier than outside, the slow gurgling bubble of long, open minnow tanks making it seem like we're all breathing under water. I brace for the dumbfounded looks, the guffaws—*Fly fish?* But one of the old guys rubs at his jowls and says, "Grandpa's Creek's got some brookies up high. I suppose you could use flies up there."

His pal asks, "Know why they call it Grandpa's?"

I shake my head.

"'Cause Grandpa never told nobody where it was neither."

That one's so old even his partners can't muster up more than a tired grin.

I return my own sick smile. "I got a boy out in the truck that's living down here now. I'm just trying to set him up with a spot he can fish."

The first one, the jowl rubber, eyes me a second. "Your boy?"

I nod.

"Living down here, and you not?"

I nod again.

He asks where I'm from, then gives a low, sorrowful whistle, shaking his head. Then, slowly, he pulls some scrap paper from beneath his counter. He starts scratching out directions to Grandpa's Creek. "While you're at it," he says, pointing behind me at a tiny pegboard holding half a dozen cork poppers, "pick up a few of those. There's bass around that should make him forget trout." He flips over his paper and draws out directions for a couple bass spots.

Pushing his map across the counter to me, he asks, "He got hisself a new daddy now?"

"A new . . ." I stutter, the idea striking like a hammer. "No. No. Nothing like that."

"Well, if he lives close, you send him here if there's anything he needs. Wave a fly around sometimes myself."

I reach for the map, still a little sick at the idea of Kenny adopting a replacement for me.

Jowls pins it to the counter. "Them popper's a buck apiece." He smiles. "Gonna give up Grandpa's, gotta turn a profit."

I buy four of them, the bank account squealing.

We get in to Grandpa's too late to try it that night. Just stuff down a few more baloney sandwiches, munch an apple as a substitute for toothbrushing, and crawl into our bags in the back of the truck.

Lying there side by side in the dark, leaves rustling thickly around us, a few stars poking through, I ask Kenny if he's okay. "Snug as a bug," he answers, and I smile.

"Where do you suppose Mom thinks we are now?" he asks.

I wait, but guess he needs an answer. "Halfway down the Dearborn, I suppose."

"Just after that rapid," he answers. "But before the rock garden. There's that one hole where the river esses left, then right. With the boulder in the middle of it. We could be camped there."

He sees it as clearly as I do.

"Remember that rainbow I caught there?"

Though most of my fish have blended together, I find I still remember almost all of his as individual events. "Sure," I say. "I remember. A wild leaper."

"That was a good one," he says, soundly pleased and sleepy.

I wait, but he doesn't say anything more.

"You know, Kenny. Your mom and I used to camp out like this. We used to sleep in the back of the truck. Cook over fires. She knows that spot on the Dearborn as well as you do."

I wait for an answer but he's asleep, which I guess I knew, even waited for. That's all true, about his mom and me, and, thinking of how I haven't let him call her, it takes me forever to drift off myself. I wind up whispering to the night, all sorts of stories about Carly and me I know I should tell him someday; let him see his mom and his dad out camping and fishing, stretching beneath the stars in our sleeping bags just like this. Snug as bugs.

First thing the next morning, before coffee, or oatmeal, or anything at all, we start to fish Grandpa's, fish with hope for the first time since we left his mother.

And Jowls wasn't lying. The brookies come up just like they do in the beaver ponds back home. Small and scrappy, striking just about whatever hits the water. I catch one, then leave my rod in the truck and follow Kenny around, watching him, a prodigy with the rod. He asks if we can keep some for breakfast, and I say, "That old guy did us a favor sending us here. We better not."

Then I wonder what I could have been thinking. I say, "Of course we can keep a few, Kenny. That's a great idea. They'll make about the best breakfast going."

But Kenny lays down his line, waits, then strikes perfectly to hook another eight-inch bundle of angry trout. As he strips it in, he shakes his head. "No," he says. "You were right the first time. This is that old guy's place."

I shut my eyes to keep from seeing what we've done to Kenny, how he's playing the grown-up here. I hear him release the fish, his standard "Go on, you shrimp, tell your dad we're here."

We fish all morning, our stomachs rumbling, until finally the brookies settle down, tired of throwing themselves onto our hooks.

"You should've kept fishing," Kenny tells me on the way back to the truck.

"I fish plenty," I answer. "Sometime it's more fun to watch."

He gives me a doubtful glance and breaks down his rod, sliding it carefully back into the tube. I'm already pumping the stove, dying to eat something, even the packets of too-sweet instant oatmeal.

"I'm going to leave that rod with you," I tell him as I strike the match, adjust the gush of loose flame. "All your stuff. Flies, vest, all of it. This can be your place, too, now."

"How would I ever get here?"

"It's not that far. We've kind of been driving in circles."

"Am *I* supposed to drive here?" he asks.

And finally I see what he means. His mother isn't going to break any bones in her rush to get him back fishing, the one thing the two of us always did together.

I'm trying to think of some solution, at least something to tell him, when he asks, "Did Mom really used to go fishing? Does she really know that spot on the Dearborn?"

I shoot him a glance, but he's just watching me open faced, waiting. You little faker, I think, lying there listening the whole time, concentrating on keeping your breathing slow and loud, not missing a word. Then I see him in his new bedroom, his little string clenched in his fist, breathing that way until his mother closes the door on him after the last check, then rising up to practice his bowlines and blood knots.

"Did she?" he asks again.

I nod. "When we first knew each other. We floated all the time. She never fished that much, but she loved the water. Loved moving on it. Seeing everything."

"How come she doesn't anymore?"

I dip my old blackened pot into the creek, hear the outside hiss dry when I put it over the flame. "I don't know," I say. "People change." I'm quoting something she once told me, but if there's an answer lamer than that, I wouldn't want to hear it.

"How come?" he whispers.

What can I tell him? That when he was a baby we couldn't float without leaving him with someone, which felt too much like neglect for us to do it more than just that once, when all we did was row so we could get back home? That after a few years off the water everything snowballed, that we could never understand how we'd had that much time in the first place? How we lost that big piece of us first, and the other pieces, big and small, just kept flaking off, leaving us chipped and exposed, both different from anything we'd ever imagined becoming? How scary it'd gotten, the anger we couldn't understand and couldn't stop?

And, without crushing him with the weight of all that, how do I explain that just watching him let go those little slivers of fish, I realized that if that was the cost of him—everything Carly and I gave up, even each other—it was a bargain, a price I'd pay again in a heartbeat? That I'd throw my own heart into the deal all over again?

I chew on my lip and watch the flames, the little strings of bubbles writhing up the sides of the old pot.

"How come?" he asks again, patient as a rock. "How come she doesn't go anymore?"

I shake my head. "I don't know," I say, a lie meant to spare him, but that leaves me bloodied. "I wish I did. I wish I could have stopped it. That we could still . . ."

I'm tasting blood, my lip ground between my teeth, and I turn away, looking for the bowls, the little packets of that disgusting oatmeal.

Kenny touches my leg. Just a tiny pat, a little fading stroke, and I wonder what it's cost him, his comforting his dad, as if there were a Band-Aid big enough to heal us all.

"We gag down this stuff," I say, having to clear my throat. "We gag it down, and we'll head back to town. Give your mom a call. Let her know we're all right."

He nods, and I wonder if he really thinks we are all right. If we ever will be.

I sit in the truck while Kenny makes the call from one of those little round phone booths that don't give you any privacy, any protection from the elements. The windows are down and I study Jowls's maps to his bass holes, trying not to listen to Kenny, but unable to stop myself when I hear him say, "The Dearborn was the best, Mom! Dad says it's still just like it was the last time you went."

He listens a moment, says "Uh huh" a few times, and I glance over, see the phone huge against his head, the gap between the mouthpiece and his lips, which move as he silently mouths her words, a habit he's had since he was a toddler, the very first time he talked on a phone.

He shakes his head to some question, then answers, "We're in Choteau. We just ate at that restaurant with the wagon wheels on the roof." A pause. "Pancakes. Dad let me get a full stack." Another pause and a smile. "All of them," he brags.

"We're going up the Sun now. Dad just wanted me to call to let you know we're okay."

He listens a long time, nodding and whispering to himself. Then he says "Okay," several times in a row. Then "Me, too," and I know she's told him she loves him, and I know she means it with all her soul.

He says "Okay" once more, but then quick, maybe even while she's lifting the phone off her shoulder, probably crying, he blurts, "Mom?"

He's in time. He smiles. He says, "Where do you think we should camp tonight?"

He listens, then says "Okay" once more, and "Thanks," and then, "Me, too, Mom. Uh huh. Really, Mom. Okay. Good-bye."

He walks slowly back to the truck, not quite meeting my eyes, suddenly suspecting that I heard every word. He jumps up onto the seat and pulls his seat belt around himself.

I flatten Jowls's map between us, over the atlas that's been there since I left Montana. "This place looks pretty close," I say, pointing. "I think we'll be able to find it."

Kenny nods. He says, "Mom says we should camp up at Benchmark, on the South Fork of the Sun. She says it should be pretty this time of year, but that the water will be ice cold and for you to buy me waders and not let me go out over my knees. She says to watch out for bears. There's grizzlies there, she says. She says you know the spot."

I nod as if everything we've done, everything he's just said, makes perfect sense. "I do," I answer.

The Net

We were married at dawn, a time more rightfully reserved for executions. It was outdoors, of course, the Tetons all rosy, the knob of hill we stood on just higher than the thick white mist clotting the paths of the Buffalo and the Snake. Beautiful, but with the guests rubbing sleep from their eyes, the September chill shrinking everybody into their coats and fine clothes, we all looked pretty rumpled. Everybody except Dalton, who worked on the river and was always up before dawn anyway. We'd spent hours and hours composing our vows (he had anyway) but when it came right down to it, I could only mumble mine, my lips and tongue thick and slow with sleep and cold.

All I wanted to do was crawl back into bed. With Dalton or without, I didn't care. If I'd been awake, I couldn't have been happier, but suddenly I felt less like a bride than a character from some old movie: blindfolded before the firing squad, bull's-eye pinned over my heart.

When Dalton's friend Jonna (a nurse *and* a preacher in some religion I'm pretty sure she invented herself) pronounced us a couple, Dalton and I walked down the hill onto the flat, heading for the water. Instead of rings, which, besides being an archaic sign of ownership, Dalton said, were the source of countless open-pit cyanide-leach gold mines gutting the mountains and trashing the rivers— though I wouldn't have minded a little diamond—we were going to dip our hands in the river, let it run around our wrapped-together fingers, joining us on a journey as long as the water's, a cycle, Dalton said, that's bigger and more eternal than any ring. He can really get going on that kind of thing, and I usually don't mind, though that time I couldn't help wondering how something can be *more* eternal.

But as soon as we were on the flat, the frost sweeping onto my long dress, his black pants, my ridiculous shoes soaked through in an instant, negotiating frost-heaved bunchgrass and river rock instead of some church aisle's red carpet, the morning fog enveloped us and suddenly, rather than starting on some long journey together, it seemed like we'd lost our way. Nobody in the crowd was going to follow us down that bank, and that fast it seemed like Dalton and I'd not just tied our two lives together, but that we'd cast off the rest of the world. Believe me, though the cold had already turned me into one gigantic goose bump, I got a whole new run of them then.

We did the water thing anyway—unbelievable water can be that cold and still flow—then Dalton turned to me and blew out this sigh like he hadn't been able to draw a breath all morning. "Holy shit," he said. "We did it." Mister Philosopher. Just can't beat the romance out of him.

How about *You are the most beautiful bride in the world.* Something like that? *You've made all my dreams come true.* So I answered, "Holy shit, you don't know how close you are to starting your journey with a swim."

He blinked a couple of times, and I started to say, "You don't just say Holy Shit to . . . you don't . . . that should not be the first thing out of your mouth to your new . . ." But I gave up. Watching him watching me, trying to figure me out, trying to find what he'd done to me, to himself, I wound up shrugging, then giving him a hug. He was so warm it felt good, downright lifesaving, and I whispered, "Holy shit, we did it all right."

We stayed there a long time, holding each other, finally warming up. I kept my eyes closed, hoping the fog would burn off, that when I opened them again the Buffalo would stretch out before us, the fall-scorched cottonwoods and willows burning bright in the first touch of sun. Finally somebody on the knob above us honked a car horn, and clear as a bell you could hear somebody laugh and snort, "You asshole." Dalton's pals.

Dalton whispered, "They're probably freezing," and then he added, and I will always love him for this, "I know I am."

I answered, "No shit," just to keep with his lingo for the morning. Giving a stage shiver, though staging was hardly necessary, I added, "Whose idea was this anyway?" knowing it was both of ours. We turned then, me finally opening my eyes just to find the fog as thick as ever, a frosty dense mist around us. But when we crawled back up the hill we broke into sun, and the waterways below us were suddenly beautiful, bright pathways just waiting for the two of us.

Coffee and doughnuts sat stacked to the ceiling in one of the vans, and we all chatted and chewed, circling our fingers around our cups, greedy for the heat. Everybody was so glad for the sun they practically giggled. Dalton and I took turns in the other van, changing out of our wedding finery—more archaic tradition, Dalton said, though I'd insisted. When we came out we looked just like everybody else in the valley, bulky with layers of fleecy synthetic pile, neoprene waders, but for a few minutes there we'd been our parents, Mom's dress fitting me so much like a skin it was spooky.

I walked straight to her and buried my face in her shoulder. I wanted to say something so profound, so deep, and as usual I cut right to the chase, starting to cry, choking out nothing more than "Oh, Mom."

We'd dragged them out from Ohio for this, and under one of Dalton's spare rain jackets I knew Mom was wearing my favorite outfit, long out of style, and that she'd done that only for me, that never before had she been caught so behind the fashion. She held me tight and whispered, "Don't worry about the dress, honey." Meaning the wedding dress, that she'd salvage it somehow, that dragging it through the wilderness here hadn't ruined it beyond her ability to repair anything, that though she didn't understand anything about this, about anything Dalton and I would ever do, *our entire generation* I could almost hear her sigh, she would be a good sport and rise above it, always there to pick up the pieces. I could picture the What-can-you-do? shake of her head at bridge club, hear the rattle of her long earrings—*And, for their honeymoon, they've taken off on some fishing trip!* All sorts of old heads wagging in sympathy, someone saying, *Well, in our day, there was still something left for the honeymoon.* Though I loved her to pieces, I suddenly wondered how it had felt so comfortable to feel like I was becoming more like her. I stopped crying, and she let go of me at the same time I let go of her.

Dad, I was afraid, would stick out his hand, offer me a hearty handshake, but when I stood in front of him, he was the one with tears in his eyes, and he swallowed me in a bear hug I could barely remember from childhood. "You take care, Maddy," he said to me, then said it again. "You take care."

"I will, Daddy," I said, wanting to say something reassuring, something like, "Jeez, Dad, we got *married*. It's not like we're jumping off a cliff or anything." But I heard a scrape of gravel then, a grunt of effort, and looking over Dad's shoulder I saw Dalton and his buddies lift our raft off the ground, starting to haul it down the hill to the river, and it felt more like a cliff dive than anything else. Whoever invented this wedding-day emotional ride must have been the same guy who drew up the first roller-coaster.

There were a lot of cheers and bon voyages as Dalton and I settled into our places on the raft; beside each other, one on each oar—more of Dalton's light-touch symbolism, but an impossible way to row a boat. As soon as we turned the first bend one of us would have to really take the oars and the other would unpack the rods and start to fish. We'd side stepped mentioning who'd do which first.

But I knew other symbolism: Vikings casting off the boat with the body of their fallen hero, letting it drift out, an oceangoing bier. Or was it a pyre? We drifted away, people growing quiet, waving instead of shouting. Until the mist folded around the two of us in our boat, I kept my eyes peeled for any of Dalton's buddies who might lob a funereal torch.

The quiet then, in the fog alone, was eerie. I kept waiting for the gunning of engines behind us, another har-har-har honking of horns. But they waited, letting us sneak off like we really were the only people in the world. It must have been my parents, standing there looking so serious, so old, that held Dalton's crew in that kind of check.

But finally one of them just couldn't stand it anymore, no matter the look my mom must have skewered him with. As Dalton and I eased alone through the fog, their old war cry suddenly shook down the river after us. "She's in the net!"

I stiffened, sitting beside Dalton at my oar, peering downstream at the snaggletoothed mess of snags and bars splitting the river. Only after the echo faded did we look at each other. It was a shout from some old fishing show they'd watched when they were growing up, if you could really say they ever grew up. I must have heard it bellowed over a hundred fish, a hundred dropped eight-balls, a thousand crushed beer cans. "I am not in anybody's net," I hissed to Dalton. "Yours or anybody's."

"I know." Dalton grinned. "Why don't you start fishing?"

"Don't think I can handle the oars?" I snapped, and before I could clap my hand over my mouth, stop the words, Dalton was paler than he'd been an instant before, his summerlong tan bleached to a February pallor.

I gasped, "My God! An hour in that dress and I've become my mother."

"I didn't sign up to marry your mom," Dalton stammered.

"Me either," I answered. "I mean to be her. I mean, I'm not her, Dalton."

"Why don't I start fishing then?" he whispered.

He didn't wait for whatever might come out of my mouth next. Just left his oar so fast I had to snag it before it slipped through the lock. He had his back to me then, unscrewing the cap to his rod case. I spun us around to a decent ferry angle, a relief to have a hand on each oar after those few uncoordinated moments of only holding one, not knowing what the other might do.

We slipped by a huge snag, a hoary old root pad tapering down through its weather-beaten, spiral-grained trunk, speckled white with merganser shit. The hole it'd dug was filled mostly with gravel this late and low, but Dalton worked out just enough line to set down a Blue-Winged Olive. It was, I knew, the last fly he'd used on our trip up to the Henry's Fork.

Such a dainty fly was a long, long shot here, and Dalton knew it. He cast again, maybe waiting for me to say the first thing that would set my mother adrift, Captain Bligh her to the vast expanses without us.

"Maybe a little bead-head would work better," I tried. "Maybe under a Stimulator. Even a big Humpy."

"Could be," he answered, casting again.

One little slip from me, I saw, and he was hard into a pout. Mister Outdoorsman/Western/Waxed-Mustache/Poet-at-Heart/Boatman Extraordinaire. The big crybaby.

"Look," I said, "I'm sorry. It just popped out. The way you said that about fishing first. I can handle a raft fine."

"I know. I was only asking if you wanted to fish. I was going to let you do it first."

"Fine," I said. "Thank-you. But as long as you *are* doing it first, the least you could do is try."

So before we knew it we were into a cutthroat, down-and-dirty, who-catches-more/bigger/better/faster fishing competition. Like kids. "Nah, nah, my fish is bigger than your fish." Unbelievable. Married forty, fifty minutes and we'd come to this.

He rigged a bead-head under a Stimulator—now where did he get that idea?—and it was only a few casts before I edged him by a pretty hole and he hooked into his first, on the Stimulator, and, as he crowed, it was "A man-eater!" A nice cutthroat he claimed broke twenty inches. Went maybe seventeen. At the outside.

We switched seats and, just to be fair, I rigged up exactly the same combo. He rowed like he would for a client, giving me every chance, but it wasn't until we hit one of the rare long, calm straightaways, where there wasn't much hope of anything, that my Stimulator disappeared.

I struck back, something solid as a rock tied into my bead-head. Seemed hardly to move, then, slowly, it sank away and turned downstream. At first the line barely pulled out, then it started chugging along, finally smoking downriver. Like a big old locomotive, Casey Jonesing it up to full steam.

I tightened my fingers against the unwinding spool, taking an instant to flash Dalton a look, but he just grinned back at me, not sulking about losing the first round so quick. I gave him a quick one back, then turned to matters at hand.

The backing was showing, though I never actually got into it. A few wraps of Day-Glo orange fly line left. And then my monster, record-shattering, contest-clinching trout—it had to be a brown—just gave up the ghost. I started cranking in quick, then even faster, just to keep some tension on the line.

"Maybe its heart exploded," Dalton whispered.

I was feeling a little sick, guessing that Dalton was guessing the same thing I was guessing. Even before I saw the first scaly flash of dirty brown-gold. Whitefish.

As I brought it to hand, Dalton said, "Snouter?"

I nodded, working the tiny hook out of the blob of cartilage that served as mouth and nose and bottom grubber all at once.

"Looks like a trophy one," Dalton said. I didn't know if he was rubbing my nose in it or only making a peace offering. Either way, I didn't much care for it. Everybody knows whitefish don't count.

As carefully as if it was a fabled trout, I eased the ugly stepsister back to freedom.

Then sitting up and turning to fix Dalton with a glare, I said, "Look, did you even once consider telling me I was the most beautiful bride in the world today?"

"What?" he blurted.

"Did you?"

"You? Tell *you* something like that?"

"Well, if I'm that goddamn hideous, why did you marry me?"

"Oh, I see," Dalton said, tugging on his chin the way he does. So cerebral. "We based this all on personal appearance."

"Hah!" I blurted. "If we'd done that, I'd've shaved that hokey mustache off your face years ago."

His mouth dropped open, his hand absently leaving his chin to tug at the waxed end of his prized facial hair.

I couldn't keep in a chuckle, same way I never could as a kid, caught red-handed in something mean and nasty, all the wrong things sneaking out of me. I kept staring at him, challenging only because I didn't know how to say I was sorry, didn't know what was wrong with me, why I kept being this way.

But Dalton was too stunned to do anything but gape back at me, not all that different looking from that poor old pooped-out whitefish.

"It's just that," I finally tried to start. "I don't know. It's just that, you know, your wedding day. I'd always had this picture, you know? Cathedrals and all. The whole rice-throwing, tin-can-dragging, threshold-carrying thing, the fear and surprise and waiting finally over."

"I wouldn't say the fear and surprise have quite played out of this one," Dalton managed to whisper.

And that, for some reason, just cracked me up. I laughed way too hard, winding up holding my ribs and sucking air like a bank-tossed sucker.

The next thing I knew we were nudging the shore, Dalton petting my forehead as I tried to get my breath back, wipe away the tears. "You are you know," he whispered. "The most beautiful, I mean. I just thought that if I ever said anything like that, well, you know. I thought you'd brain me."

I thought, *My God, this guy doesn't even know me!* but I answered, "Probably. Any other day, probably. But this is different. We did something huge today, Dalton."

"You're telling me?"

I stared out at the gently roiling water, the straightaway breaking into a right-hand bend, a gravel bar splitting off a skimpy side channel on the inside. "I wish there was a goddamn threshold out here someplace," I said.

Fighting the fish, the whole morning on the roller-coaster ride, had finally cleared the cobwebs out of my head, and I looked hard at Dalton, his silly mustache trembling on the verge of a smile.

"If there was, I'd carry you over it, Maddy."

"Really?" I asked, truly wanting to know, not just some spoiled princess wanting reassurance. I was thinking of our vows, how I'd let Dalton have his say on almost every line. Instead of saying "I do," which Dalton said was a ridiculous promise in the face of everything that could happen, every bit of it unknown, we had answered our pseudopreacher with "It is my strongest desire."

"Of course," Dalton answered, starting to slip an arm under my shoulders, like he was going to carry me across any damn thing right now if it'd get us past this.

"Is that your strongest desire?" I asked. "To carry me over something?"

He grinned, starting to lift. "You bet it is. Over everything."

"What kind of flannel-mouthed, waffling, New Age crap is that?" I snapped. "'My strongest desire.' Hell, my strongest desire two minutes ago was to tie into a fish that'd dwarf yours, that'd make me king of this boat. And now yours is to stumble me over some chunk of old driftwood, 'Get that out of the way.'"

"That's not what I meant," he started.

"Look!" I interrupted. "Skip the 'desire' shit. We're going to desire just about everything before our run is through. Hell, we've got a pretty good jump on that already. What I want to know is do you really want to marry me right this instant? Right now! Mom and all! You want on this roller-coaster or not?"

Dalton swallowed. His arm was still around me, but he wasn't trying to lift me anywhere anymore. The mist had left a little sparkly dew all across the top of his shoulders.

"And I am not in anybody's net!" I insisted, tears trickling down my cheeks, which only made me furious. I took a nasty swipe at them with my fist all balled up, just as Dalton bent low to kiss me, whispering, "I do." Nearly knocked his block off.

He sat down on the cobble, rubbing at his cheek.

I rubbed at my own cheeks, at my eyes. "Sorry," I said. "I didn't mean to hit you. That was an accident."

"Are you sure?" he asked.

"Of course I'm sure."

"Okay," he said, tugging at his chin. "You're positive?"

"Yes, I'm positive."

"Really?"

"The idea's getting tempting, Dalton."

"Okay," he said again. "Well then, 'I do.'"

"Not just the moment's strongest desire?"

"The moment's strongest desire is to be like we've always been. Not like this."

"This is part of it."

"Not the part I most strongly desire."

I couldn't help a smile. "No," I said. "Me neither."

"So what is?" Dalton asked. "What is your moment's strongest desire?" He stood back up, sat beside me on the raft.

"To get back on the water, I guess. Start this journey of ours all over again."

"It's a long way to Wilson," Dalton said, which for him was agreeing and surrendering at the same time. I'd booked us into a bed-and-breakfast there. It'd be a long float, not a lot of dawdling for fishing, but Dalton had originally, during the vow-composing days, suggested we camp out, spend days on the river alone.

But I'd drawn the line there. We could get married at the crack of dawn on some deserted riverside hilltop, we could bundle into our waders and layers, we could spend the days fishing and floating, but we were going to sleep in beds, nice ones, that we didn't have to make in the morning, and we were going to have breakfasts fixed for us, gourmet stuff, and we weren't going to wash the dishes, not squat scrubbing sand around some oatmeal bowl in some stream that'd freeze the tusks off a walrus.

Dalton pushed the boat off, and, when we began to just drift, neither of us at the oars, I thought how much like marriage this was going to be. Wondering who the hell is steering, how you're ever going to get around all those wicked-ass snags, what's going to keep you from beaching on those long, gray, dry gravel bars.

I bit my lip till I thought it'd bleed, and Dalton finally said, "You caught the last one," leaving it up to me.

I stood, keeping low, and crawled back to the oars. We were all right for a second, though, just starting into the top of the lazy turn, and I left the oars shipped.

"Unless you want to say whitefish don't count," Dalton suggested. "Then it'd still be your turn."

"They count," I answered. "It's all going to count, Dalton. Snout trout and squawfish. Even suckers. Not just the big bad browns."

He grinned and said, "Well, we're even then. One species apiece." He started working out line, his false casts arcing his hooks back and forth over our heads.

Dalton let his flies down an inch or so from the bank. He peered after them, ready to strike, and I pushed my oars into the water.

Home Before Dark

My stepson, Gordon, was already in the café when I got there and he poured coffee for me as I sat down. He added my cream and sugar without asking, though sugar was something I'd given up a long time ago. I stared at him while he stirred the cream. We'd had dinner the night before, with our wives, but I'd spent the night watching Sandy, my wife—his mom—worried about how she was holding up.

We ordered a quick breakfast, and because I couldn't think of anything to say, I asked, "When's the last time you went fishing?"

"Years ago. Monique isn't much of an outdoorsman. I wish she would've come, though. She was pretty nervous last night, but you'd like her if you got to know her."

"I'm sure of that," I said conversationally, but Gordon gave me a quick glance, a questioning look I remembered. "If you picked her to stick with she must be a good one," I said, and it sounded as false as it was.

Gordon answered, "You're the one who picked well."

"I tried to get your mom to come along," I told him. "But she thought it would be nice if just the two of us went."

"Old times' sake."

I nodded, though Sandy had stayed home thinking I might get some answers out of him alone. We looked away from each other as the food was set down. After the waitress left, I took a deep breath but wound up only asking something harmless, like "What have you been doing?" or "Where'd you and Monique meet?"

And Gordon responded with the same light chatter. We argued over the bill when it came and I didn't mention his mother again until we were taking the canoe off the car, explaining that Sandy and I had run the shuttle last night. After we settled the canoe into the river, Gordon stood beside it, staring out over the flow of dark water. Dawn was late with the fall, and it was just growing light. Scattered flocks of geese struggled by overhead, barely visible, honking mournfully. The air was much colder than it had been yesterday, wafer-thin ice rimming the stones against the bank.

"Thanks for showing this to me again," Gordon said, shivering, huddling deeper into his coat. If it'd been years and years ago, I would've run my hands up and down his sides, quick and hard, chasing away goose bumps. But I just stood quietly on the bank and watched him shiver.

"Ready?" I asked.

"And waiting," he answered, his old line.

I paddled from the stern, and Gordon was quick to strip out line and begin casting. But he was wearing big goofy mittens, city things, and it was nearly impossible for him to hold his line. He laughed about it, and I asked if he wanted my fingerless gloves.

He shook his head without turning around and said, "I've just got to toughen up is all. I've forgotten about so much." He took off his mittens then and started casting for real. I'd forgotten how graceful he was, and I stopped paddling to watch him quarter the nymph upstream and work it across the current.

"You haven't forgotten a thing," I said.

"That's not what I expected to hear from you," he responded. He did turn then, his old challenging smile bold across his face.

"Forgotten a thing about fishing."

He waited for me to go on, his smile starting to quaver the way it did when he was in trouble as a kid, trying so hard to show he didn't care. I watched him turn away, picking up his rod, and I told myself again that I was glad to see him, glad to see him hug his mother again. But I also knew I'd never be able to forget how he'd just disappeared, how he'd left her wondering for six years. During those years I'd never doubted that we'd see him again, and I kept reassuring Sandy, whispering things about adolescent rage, the difficulties of leaving the nest, the whole time picturing that smug smile of his, wondering if I'd be able to keep from punching it from his face when he reappeared.

He had a strike then, and I've rarely been so happy to see one. His face lit up, and he lifted the rod tip just quickly enough to set the hook without pulling it away. The trout was a native, a cutthroat, not too big, and it gave up quickly. Gordon dipped his hand into the icy water, freeing the hook, releasing the fish just as I said, "Awful nice pan size."

He looked down into the water. "I never liked killing them," he said.

"What are you talking about? We ate rivers of trout. Your mom loves them."

"That was before I knew there were so many ends to things."

Gordon looked at me, and I was shocked by the startling familiarity of his face. I remembered the odd gold bursts flecking his brown eyes. When he was a boy they'd bothered me. They were a flaw, I thought, somehow eerie. They were too light, like sheep's eyes.

Suddenly he squinted, and I knew he was smiling his real smile. "I got the first. The biggest. The smallest. The most. I'm killing you in every category."

I'd forgotten the old contests we'd developed in the years I'd tried to gentle into his father's place. "Give me time," I said, and Gordon stripped up his slack and cast again.

We both fished as much as we could, but nothing else struck before the river curved and I had to put down my rod for my paddle. Gordon retrieved his nymph, too, but instead of picking up a paddle to help, he stuck his hands under his arms.

"It's funny how whenever I thought about all this it was always the fish I remembered, and the way the river looked when the mist was just clearing. Or the way you'd get so tense going through white water, how it wasn't safe to say anything then, but afterward whatever I said was the funniest thing in the world. It was never the damn cold I remembered."

I glanced at the bottom of the canoe, the same one we'd used then. After he'd left I'd been able to forget he'd ever been with me, that he'd ever seen that kind of thing with me.

"It's never the damn cold I remember," Gordon said again, arms still wrapped tight around himself. "Or lugging all our stuff over those endless portages. Or sitting under the canoe during the downpours—blackfly bait."

"No one remembers the bad stuff," I said, realizing even as I spoke that that was exactly what I'd forced myself to remember about Gordon. "Why would anyone bother remembering that?"

"I think if you don't you'll wind up crazy," he answered, taking his hands out from under his arms and blowing on his fingers. "I can't even feel my fingers," he said. "You'd think I'd remember anything that hurt this much."

"It's your mind's trick. Blocking out the bad."

"It's a dirty trick," Gordon said, picking up his rod, his mom's rod, which I'd brought for him to use. He turned away from me, casting again. "If all you remember is the good, you wind up homesick for things that really weren't that great to begin with."

We were on another flat, quiet stretch, and I picked up my rod to change flies. The knot I tied took concentration. "It really was pretty great," I said quietly, beginning to understand how he'd worked things around after he left, worked them around so he could stand himself.

Gordon shrugged, facing away from me, and then nodded quickly. I could picture how he'd bite his lower lip, exactly how his cheeks would be sucked in just a little, the tightness of the lines around his golden eyes. If there wasn't the full distance of the canoe between us, I might have crawled forward then, to hug him or swat some sense into him, I wasn't sure which. But it would be dangerous now, even in the flat water, to try to make my way to him.

When Gordon had his line in, he cast out again, quartering upstream expertly. I doubted he'd forgotten a thing, no matter what he said. I began casting, too, pulling my line in whenever we reached a bend I'd have to steer through. We both started to catch fish, and I saved a few for Sandy.

The day never did warm the way it should've, and when we stopped for lunch I started a little fire. While I was building it up, when it still needed my help to keep burning, Gordon fished the hole just upstream. The glaze-thin ice had never melted off, and though there was no sun, the ice glinted white at the edge of the riffles, where the water did not move fast enough to break it.

Gordon worked the riffle, bouncing his nymph along the bottom through the broken water. I watched him pick up a fish with his first cast, then went back to work on the fire. The next time I looked he had another fish on. His breath smoked into the pinching air.

When the fire had taken hold solidly I sat beside it to watch Gordon fish. I studied him a long time, trying again to picture the sullen look of hatred we'd never understood— the look I'd thought was directed at me for replacing his father, that Sandy had thought was for her, for ever divorcing in the first place. He was intent on his fishing, and he kept at it a long while without turning to see that he was being watched. He seemed to have worked the hole out, though, and he didn't hook anything else.

Maybe it was the overcast, blocking the arc of the sun, that hid the slipping away of the day, but I sat by that fire far too long watching Gordon, while the day, and our light, kept getting shorter, the river still stretching out before us.

Finally he reeled his line in and walked back to the fire, draping three trout over the log I was sitting on. "Let's eat," he said.

He caught me looking at the dead fish and he said, "You've killed three, too. Now you can save them for Mom. She loves them."

I couldn't tell if the fish were a peace offering or if he was making fun of my murderous ways. I told him we'd save his for his mom, and I picked up my beautifully clean little trout, and we roasted them straight over coals we dragged from the main body of the fire. We ate with our fingers, and Gordon said he hadn't tasted anything like this in years. Even then, when I knew we had to get moving, we stayed over the fire, unable to draw away from its warmth, from the mesmerizing dance of the flames.

As Gordon watched the fire, I finally asked the question neither Sandy nor I had been able to manage the night before. After all, we were on the river now, and there was no place he could run. "What brings you back, Gordon?" I whispered.

Gordon didn't look up from the fire. For a long time he didn't answer. "Monique, I guess. She started it, anyway." He looked up then and smiled for a moment. "I'm glad she did, though. Some things get to seem way harder than they really are."

Somehow that shy little smile did all the wrong things, and the urge to reach across the fire and wipe it off his mouth welled up. "Six years is an awful long time," I said. "Without a word."

Gordon nodded and looked back into the last of the flames. "I know."

"We didn't even know if you were still alive. You about killed Sandy."

Gordon nodded again, a quick, guilty dip of his head. "When I left I thought that's what she was doing to me."

I looked away from him then, and when neither of us could say anymore, I walked down to the canoe for the bailing bucket. I filled it in the river and came back to douse the fire.

"We're late," I said, too fast, trying to cut him off before he could say anything else. "We stayed here too long."

"How much farther do we have to go?"

"A long way."

The water hit the fire with a screaming hiss, and great clouds of steam poured up, mixing with the leaden sky. Gordon stirred the ashes with a stick, and I poured on a second bucket. "It's dead now," he said.

"We've got to move, Gordon. We're going to have a hell of a time making it home before dark."

He nodded but stood still over the blackened sticks, watching the last of the steam trickling up. "That's what Mom always used to say. Remember that? 'Be sure to be home before dark.'"

I nodded. "She never said it much to me," I said.

"She didn't have to," he started, but before he said anything else, he pointed into the sky. "More geese."

I looked up at the tired, ragged Vs, low with the clouds. "Looking for a place to spend the night," I said.

"Already heading south?"

"It's getting that late. So are we."

"They sound sad to be leaving," Gordon said, walking to the river.

I held the canoe steady in the current while he climbed in. I pushed off and started paddling. "We really are late," I told him. "We've got to move."

Gordon picked up his paddle and started to put his back into it. I made some comment about his strength, and he started in on what his workout schedule was and all that. It was exactly the kind of mindless, friendless chitchat I'd been afraid of miring down in all day.

But Gordon stopped in midsentence, as if he'd been thinking the same thing. "Do both the geese raise their young? The male and the female?" he asked.

I opened my mouth to answer, but then guessed it really wasn't a question so much. "I don't know," I said, and we both paddled hard, watching the clouds dropping even lower, hiding the mountains the sun was setting behind.

We kept up the power as dusk wrapped around us, working too hard to speak. And then the snow began to fall, tiny white touches against our faces. "Warm enough?" I asked, and Gordon said he was fine. The snow grew steady, patient at its task, bringing on the dark even more quickly. "Are we going to get out of here before dark?" Gordon asked.

"Not a chance," I answered, thinking of Sandy watching the snow and the clock.

"What are we going to do?"

"Keep going, I guess. The river's pretty easy." But I followed the river's curves in my mind, through the looping S just before the takeout. I told Gordon about it. "There are three snags in it. Upstream one in the center, next one left, last one right. It's not hard in the light."

"Can we reach it before dark?"

"I don't know." I felt the canoe push forward a little harder with Gordon's next stroke, and I put my back into my own paddling. I knew we wouldn't make it.

Our eyes kept searching through less and less light, until finally we were guessing at shadows. Soon I realized I was listening for the bank more than trying to see it.

We both stopped paddling for a moment. "Should we get out and walk?" Gordon asked.

"I don't have a light," I said, trying to remember if I'd ever forgotten to bring one before. "We'd probably get lost. At least I know where the river goes."

I could hear Gordon cut his wooden blade into the water, and we began to paddle again, my ears straining against the blinding darkness.

"Is this dumb?" Gordon asked. "Are we going to kill ourselves out here tonight?"

"Of course it's dumb."

"I knew it would be," he said, but then I began to hear a faint rise in the hissing of the water. I said, "We may be there." I reached out with my paddle and it touched against the bank.

Gordon said, "The snags?"

The hiss was a rushing sound now, and I said, "Yes. If you can see the first one, go hard left after it."

"I can't see a thing."

"Well, hear. If you can hear it."

We were quiet then, and the rushing grew louder. It seemed to be in the right place. I held my paddle out to the bank once more, measuring, remembering the snags. The blade scraped harshly against the gravel, and the air around us erupted.

The explosion of honking startled me so badly it was a moment before I realized they were geese, hundreds of them struggling up from the banks. The wind whistled and whisked through their wings. Their honking battered my ears, as if they screamed warnings, unable to believe I couldn't hear. I thought if I reached up perhaps they would lift me off this river, over the snags ahead.

I felt Gordon pulling hard to the left up front, and though I could hear nothing but the geese I drew hard that way, too.

Then the canoe brushed something on the right, lifting and listing, and I thought we were going over. There was a flash of lighter water on that side and the canoe righted itself, and we were through before I knew we'd started. The geese and the rush of water faded behind us, and I could hear Gordon breathing hard up front.

"Did we make it?" he whispered. "Were those the snags?"

"Those were the snags."

"We hit the last one, didn't we?"

"Grazed it."

"Are there any more? Was that the last of it?"

"That's all," I said, my heart only now beginning to speed up, battering at my ribs as I pictured the two of us tumbling alone through the black, icebound current.

Gordon said something else, but we broke through another flock of geese. They sounded as if they were in the boat, and I could feel individual birds going over my head. Once I heard the hard flutter of braking wings, and a heavy gust of air hit my cheek. When they faded downstream, Gordon said, "One of them touched me. On my face."

"I thought they were going to carry us away."

"What will they do now? How will they land in the dark?"

"I don't know."

"They don't have to keep flying until it gets light, do they?"

He sounded so distressed I said "No," though I didn't have any idea what they could or could not do. "They can land at night. They can feel how close they are to the ground."

"Really?" he asked, and I said, "Sure."

"I wish I could've done that," he said, and we kept moving downriver, occasionally touching the banks with our paddles to make sure we were still there. Gordon said it was like float-

41

ing through space, and if he couldn't touch the bank, he wouldn't even know he was on the planet. "Maybe we didn't make it through the snags," he said. "Maybe this is our afterlife."

"No," I said. "We wouldn't be here without your mom. I wouldn't be."

"Or Monique. Monique would be with me."

I waited for him to say "And Mom," but he didn't do that. I said, "What did you think about when we started to tip back there? Who did you think about?"

"Monique," he answered, too fast, before he could have given it any thought. Then he blurted, "She's pregnant. That's what I thought about. That's why she made me come here to see Mom."

I didn't say anything. I'd wanted him to say *Sandy*, but I could see now why that wouldn't be true.

Then Gordon said, "That's all I ever think about now. I walk around scared to death. Scared about things I'd never even thought of."

I laughed a little, vengefully, but Gordon ignored me. "Does that ever leave? Even when you've taken all the tests? Even when you know the baby is all right? Isn't the fear supposed to go away?"

The moon had come up behind the clouds and I could see the faintest outline of Gordon against the sky, and I told him that the fear goes away, although I really didn't know much about it. Gordon was my only experience at being a parent, and he'd been ten years old when we'd met. But I remembered getting up on nights as dark as this to stand in his doorway, listening for his breathing, and I doubted that the fear ever disappeared completely. No test was that foolproof.

"Why won't mine go away, then? My fear?"

"Maybe it changes more than goes away. Becomes more awe than fear."

"Just the thought of being a dad scares me," Gordon whispered. "What if you do your best and they turn out like me?"

There was no answer for that, and we paddled until suddenly the takeout was there, appearing as quickly as the water cut by the snags. I pulled over, and the canoe scraped the gravel. I said, "End of the line."

Gordon stayed in his seat. I could see his outline in the river now, the water holding the light of the clouds. I held my hand out. I don't know how he saw it in the dark, but he took it and I pulled him up out of the canoe. Once he was on the bank, we let go of each other.

"We've got to move. We're probably scaring Sandy to death."

We picked up the canoe and carried it toward my truck. "Does she worry about you now? Does she tell you to be home before dark?" Gordon asked.

"Of course," I said. "She loves me."

"So there's nothing left for you to fear, is there?"

"Losing that."

"Doesn't that scare you to death? All by itself?"

"No," I said, wondering if that was true. "You can't start missing the greatest thing in the world before it's even gone." I paused, trying to remember his words. "You'd wind up crazy if you did that."

We lifted the canoe onto the truck, and when I walked around for the tie-downs I bumped into Gordon in the dark. I felt the sticky touch of the fish he'd killed for his mother. He stepped quickly backward and I could feel him staring at me. "She'll love those fish," I said.

"I'm sorry," he said. "About leaving. About everything. I was such a mess then."

His words brushed against my face like the startled rush of a goose wing. I told him his mother had known that all along but that if he could bring himself to tell her, it would be like one of those wondrous tests they had now, the ones Monique had taken, that really assured nothing but meant so much anyway.

Natives, Boxcars, and Transplants

At first it was too dark, but even after the sun came up traffic was pretty thin. It's not like I ever figured hitchhiking with a canoe was going to be easy. I did figure my chances would be better standing up, but lugging The Floating Boxcar all the way to the highway nearly killed me. Pretty soon I slipped down into the bow seat, waiting for the next pickup, or a car with racks. I carried my own tie-downs, just in case.

Of course, when me and Tarpley first saw The Floating Boxcar it wasn't The Floating Boxcar yet, and I never once figured I'd be carrying it anywhere by myself. Or carrying it anywhere, period. It was spring runoff, the water ugly and mean, and Tarpley and me were only at the river because there wasn't anything else to do. He couldn't believe I'd lived in Montana my whole life and didn't know any spring creeks or beaver dams where we could fish until the big river cleared. We spent every spare minute we had that spring searching for places to fish, even asking permission on private ground clear out to the Judiths and the Snowies, because Tarpley thought there might be undiscovered clear water someplace high like that.

But the day we found The Boxcar we were stumbling along the banks of the Missouri down by the old bridge, and Tarpley pointed to something green and flopping, stuck to the bridge's center piling. He broke into a run, already laughing.

Once we crawled over the riprap to get up on the bridge, we could see it was a Coleman canoe, what Tarpley called a peasant boat. This one was wrapped around the piling, folded in half and bucking like mad, making its own white water. Sometimes we could hear its two ends smacking against each other.

Tarpley eyed it for a while then raced back to his truck. He always had piles of stuff in the bed, and he pulled out a mess of ropes and pulleys and carabiners. He tried to explain what he was doing, but I was pretty much in the dark even when he hung over the side of the bridge far enough to work a loop around the canoe. The water gushed up his arms and though I was high and dry on the bridge I could guess how cold that muddy water was.

When Tarpley was ready, we pulled like crazy on the end of what he called a Z-rig. At first it didn't seem like we'd move anything, but suddenly the canoe squirted up the piling, the water launching it like a cork. As we drove back to Great Falls, the folded canoe rattling in the bed of his truck, Tarpley couldn't stop grinning. "We got ourselves a fishing boat, Travis!" he kept saying, though to me it looked like all we'd hauled out of the river was a trip to the dump.

But almost every night for the rest of that spring I'd finish my homework and ride my bike up to the air base where Tarpley lived, stopping at the entrance station and talking with the guard until Tarpley came and got me. Then we'd hole up in his garage, making new gunwales out of ash, scrapping the bent and twisted aluminum that Tarpley said was so cheap it made him sick. We fiberglassed the tears, and made a new runner for the floor to stiffen the wobbly plastic hull. Tarpley kept moaning about the crummy design, going on and on about the great canoes: Mad Rivers, and Blue Holes, and more.

It wasn't till we were done, when we first picked up the canoe, that we realized how heavy we'd made it. That's when Tarpley christened it The Flying Boxcar, after some huge bomber his uncle flew back in World War II.

"*Floating* Boxcar is more like it," I said. "If it does float."

But the weight didn't make any difference once we had it strapped into the back of Tarpley's truck, and we used The Boxcar a lot that summer Tarpley was here.

The first time I ever met Tarpley I was sitting by myself in the high school cafeteria. He dropped his lunch tray right next to mine. Almost without looking at me, he nodded and said, "How's it going, man?" No one in Great Falls ever said "man."

I said, "All right." He had *base kid* written all over him.

"So what's the fishing like around here?" was the next thing he asked.

After that, even though I wasn't what anyone would have called an avid fisherman, we kind of started doing stuff together. Like driving down to the river, or fixing that canoe. "Hanging," Tarpley called it.

47

I *had* fished before I met Tarpley; worms, mostly, or marshmallows, or corn. Cheese sometimes. But the first time Tarpley picked me up to go, he wouldn't even let me take my fishing stuff out of the garage. "For crying out loud," he muttered, looking over my gear. "What is wrong with you people?"

I didn't know what the problem was so I didn't say anything. One of the reasons I was Tarpley's only friend, besides him being a new guy, was that he was kind of a fanatic about some things, and I didn't want to get him started. "Come on," he said. "I got an extra rod you can use."

"I got my own rod."

"Fly rod!" he said, and, empty handed, I followed him to his truck.

That summer Tarpley taught me all there is to teach about fly fishing. I'm not saying I learned it all, but he taught it. At first he was always saying it made him just flat sick that a native Montanan, with the Missouri right outside his door, had never once picked up a fly rod. Things were always making Tarpley sick.

"Man," he told me, "we got stationed in Saudi Arabia for two years. You know what the fly fishing's like down there? About made me sick. That one about killed me."

But once I started picking up on stuff he got a big kick out of how lousy I was at it. Then finally, after I got the hang of casting and stuff, he got serious, teaching me about bugs and trout and water, all of which I'd always thought were just bugs and trout and water. I didn't have any idea there were so many kinds of each.

There was one bug that summer, a tiny, gnat-looking thing, that about put Tarpley off his head. Tricos he called them, and they came out in swarms that made me duck when The Boxcar floated through them. We caught a ton of rainbows on them. Well, Tarpley did anyway. On hooks too small to even believe. I got a few, too.

Sometimes Tarpley would let me drive his truck while he rode shotgun, going on and on about trout prey selection, and fly tying, and holding water, and whatever else popped into his head. We got out late once, Tarpley nearly wetting his pants about missing the best part of the hatch, until I finally told him to relax. "There are enough of them dang tricos to go around," I told him. We were driving through swarms of them already. They were practically greasing the windshield.

He looked at me like I had a mouthful of cow pie and didn't know it. "The hatch is already tapering off," he told me. Then before I had any idea what he was doing, he rolled down his window and stuck his face out there in the bugs, crawling out till he was sitting on the door. I reached over and grabbed his belt, struggling to drive at the same time. "Tarpley!" I shouted.

He flopped back in as quickly as he'd shot out, and he turned to me, tiny little tricos stuck here and there on his face, tangled in his hair. But where they showed best was on his teeth. Tarpley's got a pair of buck teeth you wouldn't believe. "Check the buckies, man," he said, holding his upper lip out of the way. He pulled the rearview mirror around and started counting out loud, getting only to three before wiping the bugs off.

"One and a half tricos per bucky!" he cried. "At that density we'll be lucky to catch anything."

I stared at him until I nearly drove off the road. Though Tarpley's got one of the straightest faces I've ever seen he couldn't hold it that time. He started guffawing like a mule, the way he does, and I broke up, too. "Tricos per bucky!" he snorted. "I had you going."

"You did not," I lied.

Though Tarpley knew more about fly fishing than any other human being, he'd never had a canoe before. And though I really didn't mind him teaching me about fishing, even making fun of how bad I was at it, it was kind of nice getting the hang of the canoe together. We took turns in The Boxcar's stern, slipping through little side channels, putting the sneak on fish, the guy in front doing the casting. Since most of my side-channel casts wound up in the willows, I even got a little better at steering than Tarpley did, just because I did it more.

But that fall we were in the main channel, both of us fishing the late-evening caddis hatches that had replaced the tricos, when I tied into something different from the rainbows we'd grown used to. This fish made a headlong run across the river, showing all the power of the big rainbows but none of their flash. Without even glancing back—just by hearing the sound my reel made—Tarpley stripped his line in and spun around in his seat, ready to steer.

After watching my line and getting The Boxcar started after it, he asked, "Brown?"

I shrugged. "I don't know. It's not a rainbow, though."

"Maybe a brown."

The first run didn't die until the fish ran out of room on the other side of the river. It turned upstream and Tarpley paddled like his life depended on it, grunting and swearing from the front seat, which had become the backseat now. "Into backing yet?" he asked between breaths.

"Yep," I said, wondering how he could tell from back there.

He paddled even harder then.

The fish turned at last, cutting back across the river, and I was able to get some fly line back on the reel. Tarpley slid the canoe closer to the bank and the fish seemed to brood for a while before exploding into another run.

"You know what I think?" Tarpley whispered, slaving at his paddle again.

I had my arms above my head, trying to keep the current from grabbing all the line I had out. "What?"

"I think you got a cutthroat. I think you got one of the original natives of the river."

The trout came back at us and I stripped in line like mad. "That creel survey guy said there weren't any cutthroats here anymore."

"I think you got one."

And about fifteen minutes later, after Tarpley had banked the canoe and climbed out with his net, that's exactly what we found on the end of my line. A twenty-two-inch cutthroat, all hard, bronzy gill plates, and brilliant orange throat slashes.

I walked up beside Tarpley and we each held the fish in our hands in the water, Tarpley saying that the fish was part of river history, that the cutthroat was a native, like me, and it was a good thing I'd caught it, not him.

"That's a crock," I said. "I wouldn't even know what this thing was if it wasn't for you."

Tarpley shook his head. He took the fish from me and rubbed it carefully. It stirred and he said, "It's getting ready." Then the fish was gone. Tarpley never kept anything.

"That's your fish," he said. "Now you know where it lives. You should be able to catch it again. They aren't the brightest."

"*You* know where it lives, you mean. I'll never get another crack at it now."

Tarpley didn't answer for a long time. Even though it was almost dark, and he couldn't have seen much, he just stared up to the hills behind us, what was left of a bunch of old volcanoes or something. Thin black lines of rock poked from the crests of each of the green ridges, jutting out like the scales on that one dinosaur. Tarpley always said it was one of his favorite places. We called it the Dragon's Back.

"It's your fish," he finally said. "Ready to go?"

We kept fishing that night, another of Tarpley's favorite things—trying to hook up with a fish by hearing its rise, while I strained just to see the looming shapes of the islands I steered by. And even though he caught a rainbow, the fight a ghostly listening for leaps and splashdowns, I still remember that night as the night Tarpley told me his dad had been reassigned, that he'd be moving away.

"To Kansas City," he said, sounding as if it might as well be hell. Or even Saudi Arabia.

At first I didn't say anything. I was Tarpley's only friend, but moving around as much as he had, I figured he was probably used to that. But just him saying he was going to Kansas City made me realize he was pretty much my only friend, too. I couldn't believe I hadn't thought of that before. "Are there trout there?" I asked.

"If there are, I'll find them," he answered, but he was shaking his head, like he already knew he wasn't going to find anything down there like the Dragon's Back, or The Boxcar.

"Well," I said, but couldn't think of anything to say next. I started to sing that Kansas City song, about the pretty little women they got there, but our bow scraped the gravel of the takeout before I finished a line. I don't know if Tarpley laughed or not.

We made it out a couple more times that fall, but then winter came and Tarpley was gone. He wrote in the spring, saying he'd been fly fishing for bass on some reservoir. He admitted it was fun. He added that the Missouri went right through town, but that it wasn't the same river down there— that it would make me flat sick to see it. He signed his letter *Kevin,* which I couldn't remember ever calling him. I already knew that about the Missouri, though. I'd looked it up on a map after he was gone.

Tarpley took his truck, of course, but he left The Boxcar with me, saying it was too big and heavy to ship to K.C. I didn't believe him, but he wasn't going to let me win the argument. "Use it yourself," he told me. "Catch your cutthroat again."

That's what I had in mind when I portaged The Boxcar all the way to the highway. I wasn't sure the water would be clear enough yet, but I was working at the pool that summer and the night before, when I was screening the junk off the top of the water, I found the dead tricos. Swarms of them.

I left my house at five in the morning, thinking it might take an hour just to get The Boxcar to the highway, and at least another hour to get a ride. But it took three hours to get a ride and by the time the old guy in the pickup pulled over and helped me tie in the canoe, I was frantic that I'd already missed the hatch's peak.

We drove past the Dragon's Back and I told the old guy the next exit would be perfect. That way I could float past the Dragon once I was on the river. The guy nodded, naming the put-in I wanted to use, which kind of surprised me. "That's the one," I said, looking his way just long enough to see the flies stuck in the visor in front of him. They were big hairy things, nothing like anything me and Tarpley ever used.

When we left the highway for the frontage road, the tricos started smearing the windshield, and the old guy asked, "Fly fisherman?"

"Yeah," I said automatically, but then it sounded funny. Tarpley was a fly fisherman.

"Looks like you'll have a hell of a day."

"I think we missed the best part already," I answered.

"We?"

"Me. I meant me."

I could feel the old guy looking at me, maybe waiting for me to ask him to come along or something. In The Boxcar.

And all of a sudden, because I couldn't just sit there with him waiting for me to ask that, I whipped my window down and climbed half out of it, feeling the bugs tick into my face. The guy must have thought I was going to jump. He stamped on his brakes, nearly killing me, but I still bared my teeth, which weren't half the size of Tarpley's.

When he got the truck stopped I checked the big California mirror. One trico. I slumped back into the seat, pretending I didn't see the old guy staring at me, his mouth hanging open, his Adam's apple working like one of the bobbers I used to fish with.

Before he could say whatever he was trying to say, I said, "Don't have a chance without Tarpley's buckies," which made the old guy stop trying to talk at all. He ground the truck into gear and bumped over the train tracks to the put-in. He didn't bother getting out to help untie The Boxcar. I could still feel him watching me, though, through the rear window, and I almost broke down and asked if he wanted to come along.

Instead I said "Thanks" and waved, and he rumbled up the gravel back toward the highway, leaving me standing alone beside the river, wondering if any of this by myself would even be worth putting into a letter to Tarpley.

But I strung my line and tied on a Trico Tarpley had left behind. Then I shoved off for the Dragon's Back, and that one cutthroat only me and Tarpley knew about. Once on the water, in our big, busted canoe, I started to smile. If I caught our cutthroat again, on my first time out, it would make Tarpley just flat sick.

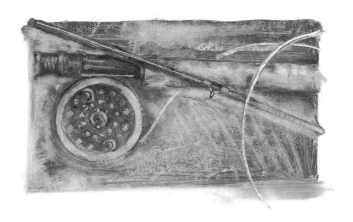

Trying to Be Normal

This is part of trying to be normal again, Corby realized, hanging on as they bounced down the rugged track through the sage. He watched his father, his hands strangling the steering wheel, though this was his idea and it was supposed to be fun. Now and then he craned forward, his chest scraping the wheel as he peered out at the dark, low sky. Corby wondered if he could really be thinking of nothing beyond getting stuck down on the river if the rain came.

In the old days Corby had watched his father drive to the paddlefish hole amazed that he didn't have to choke the wheel that way all the time. He'd cock a wrist over the top, and his hand would dangle down, half open, twisting this way and that, illustrating different points as he told his stories. They'd hit rocks or sage sometimes, and then he'd quick grab, but as soon as he had them straightened back on course, he'd go on talking, barely holding on again.

Or there was this game he had, scaring them, where he'd pretend they were completely out of control. He'd skim his hands across the wheel, one after the other, as fast as he could, pretending he was whipping it around and around, fighting it. Even when you knew it was just a trick, it was scary, and when he'd laugh and stop, you'd laugh, too, knowing you were safe and that he was driving all loose and easy.

Corby's brother, Sumner, kept trying, leaving spaces for their father to say something as he chattered about gumbo and useless tire chains, as if, at fourteen, he'd slogged alone through thousands of miles of gumbo. But their father just drove, leaving Sumner's spaces blank, as if this were a sentence to endure, not a day of fishing.

After his surprise announcement that they were going to the river at all, Corby had been the one to bring up the paddlefish rule, about no one under twelve being allowed to use the snagging rods. Their father had only answered, "Of course. Your mother didn't make the rules disappear."

Nope, Corby thought, never able to stop himself, *she's all that disappeared.* But unaccountably, his father's answer had shocked him, then only left him ashamed that the paddlefish rule had ever mattered so much. That it still did.

Leaning forward, Corby poked his head between Sumner's and his father's. "Dad, I'm gonna be twelve this fall. . . ." he began.

But his father only lifted a hand off the wheel. "Don't even start, Corby."

Sumner turned, but before he could say anything their father reached out and screwed his head back around forward. If they were alone, Corby knew, Sumner would launch into one of his scoldings, getting after him about trying to take advantage of the situation. He actually said things like that, as if he were a hundred years old, not sharing a room with him, only two grades ahead. But Corby only had to say *You're not Mom, you know,* to make Sumner attack. Then Corby would swing back wildly, blindingly happy to be brothers again.

Grinding the station wagon down the cuts in the bluff, their father ignored the scraping until they were in the dead, matted grass of the floodplain, winding their way to the bend and their paddlefish hole. There he dropped the tailgate and doled out equipment: tackle box and snagging hooks to Sumner; stout snagging rods and thin spinner to Corby; pickle bucket full of Corby's minnows and the cooler to himself.

Corby stepped carefully down the last, steep cut to the river, remembering once, when the mud had still held water, sliding down the bank again and again, exasperating his father, who'd tried to fish and keep an eye on him. He'd still talked in those days, and he'd kept warning Corby that sooner or later he'd bust his buttons on that cliff, begged him to tend his little rod, to not make him haul him back to their mother a bag of broken bones.

Past the drop, a long run of slate gray mud stretched to the edge of the water, the top dried into a wildly cracked, sharp-edged puzzle. As soon as they dropped their gear, Corby broke a chip out of the mud and flipped it at Sumner. Sumner winged one back.

"Knock it off," their father said, but no threat cut his voice.

Sumner sailed a last chip before sitting to rig the huge trebles, six feet apart, a piece of lead the size of Corby's rabbit foot at the end. Corby strung his monofilament—ten-pound test compared to the snaggers' forty—through the tiny eyelets of his rod. He pressed on a pea-sized split shot and hooked a minnow under the fin. Going through the motions.

He cast out while Sumner babbled strategy, wondering where the shelf was at this water level, where the fish would hold; all stuff Corby had heard a million times, all stuff that had nothing to do with anything. They'd just cast and cast, covering the whole place with their vicious, whistling hooks. Their father wasn't even pretending to listen anyway. Corby drove a Y-stick into the mud and dropped his rod into the notch.

Sumner and their father were casting by the time Corby dragged the cooler over to sit on. His father reared back, grunting when he powered forward and let go, sending the line screaming off the reel, the lead cannoning down almost all the way across the river, where the willow and the cotton-wood stood in a double gray line, nearly the same color as the sky.

After waiting for the lead to reach bottom his father began the retrieve, jerking back with all his might, ripping the terrible hooks through the water, hoping they struck one of the monstrous, invisible fish. He reeled in fast as he brought the rod forward, then tensed and ripped again—a motion he could repeat endlessly all day. Corby had watched so often he could have done it in his sleep.

Corby glanced at his motionless rod tip, the taut line disappearing in the oak-colored swirls. Sumner grunted, imitating their father, and Corby watched his lead splash down halfway across the river. Pathetic.

"I could do that, Dad," Corby called. "As good as Sumner."

Their father slashed back, his line striking something, and sticking. He tested the pull.

"Got the shelf?" Sumner asked, the answer obvious.

Their father ignored both of them.

"They should be holding just in front of that," Sumner tried again.

Their father backed up, bulling the lead out of the mud bank, reeling in.

"Dad?" Corby said, too close to whining.

"You're not big enough." His father grunted, arcing his line across the current to the quiet water on the other bank. "You'd wear out in nothing flat."

"I won't," Corby began, but his father let the tackle settle then threw himself into the rod, tearing the hooks through the water, searching.

Corby looked back at his own rod, the tip bobbing nervously, going still, dipping down.

"Got a nibble!" he squeaked, immediately recalling his father's quiet talk about growing up fast, having to be a man. He picked his rod carefully from the stick, getting ready, hoping he hadn't sounded babyish.

His rod tip tugged down, harder this time, and Corby struck. The drag whistled out and Corby yelled "Got one!" keeping his tip up while the line zipped through the brown water. He reeled in when he could, bringing the fish ever closer, his tongue poking from the corner of his mouth. "This isn't any goldeye!" he said once, through clenched teeth, and his father, who was coming with the net, actually laughed.

Corby spun to stare at him, but his father was already lunging with the huge, long-handled net, quicker than any snake. "Wow," he said once, the laugh already gone.

From upstream Sumner shouted, "What is it? What did he get?" He set down his rod, coming to see.

"It's a sauger!" Corby cried. "A giant one!"

Corby stared at the fat-bodied fish, pale and walleyed, thrashing in the net, mud already sticking to its sides. "Get some water, Corb'," his father said, pinning the fish to the mud with his boot while he worked at the hook.

Corby pulled the minnow bucket up, kicking at it to shake loose the bucket nested beneath. Then he ran downstream to the one spot where he could reach the water. On the way back, tipped to his side by the weight of his load, he sloshed water down his leg and over his shoes. He slid to a stop, the mud turned to grease with the slightest trace of water.

His father held the sauger up for Corby to admire, his fingers and thumb pinching its gills in hard, making its mouth gape. "Bet it goes six pounds," he said. "Haven't seen one like this out of here in years." He shoved it into the bucket, head first, its tail sticking up high.

When he'd first been allowed to go paddlefishing, Corby remembered how back at home his mother had made so much more of his little bucket of sauger than the gigantic paddlefish. When she got him alone, she pulled him tight, whispering, "They can keep their greasy old paddlefish. Sauger is my very favorite. Thank-you!"

"It won't even fit in the bucket," Corby whispered, but he didn't want to eat it now, and he wished there was some way to ask his father to let it go.

As Sumner stared at the exhausted sauger, gilling quietly in the dirty water, Corby rigged a new minnow and cast out. Sumner hadn't said a word, and Corby wondered if somehow he knew they were their mother's favorite, too. If he could be thinking the same thing.

He set his rod in the forked stick. "You never caught one that big in your life," he said, not knowing how to ask.

Sumner blinked, switching his eyes to glance at him. It took a second before he answered, "Except that twenty-pound paddlefish last year."

"That Dad made you throw back 'cause it was so small," Corby answered, wanting to scream, *That wasn't last year! The funeral was last year! The fishing season was gone before we ever thought about trying to be normal again.*

"You want Corby to snag a while?" their father asked.

Sumner jumped, headed for his rod. "Corby couldn't even cast it."

"Could too! Farther than you!"

"You wish!"

Corby stared after his brother, hoping he didn't snag anything but a stump all day. When he checked his rod tip he saw it was already dancing and he struck too quickly, wanting to have another fish on before Sumner reached his rod.

He let the weight sink back and the nibbling resumed. He waited for a harder tug and struck, crying "I got one!" again, but knowing as soon as he spoke, as he should have from the nibbling, that this time it really was only a goldeye.

Corby yanked the fish to shore, hauling it over the bank without the net. As soon as he could get the hook out, he threw the dart-shaped silver fish back into the water, but from upriver Sumner squealed, "Goldeye! Goldeye!"

Corby caught seven goldeye in a row, until his father told him to try a new spot before he ran out of minnows. Corby glared at him. He and Sumner, after all, hadn't caught a thing except that mud shelf, over and over.

Talking aloud to himself, Sumner said maybe they'd just dropped the dam release, maybe that had moved the fish, maybe they were a little early this year, or a little late. All things their father used to say.

Their father just cast and hauled, taking a step or two between casts, working the hole as if he and it were the only things left in the world.

Corby's next fish was another sauger, not as big as the first, maybe ten or eleven inches, and Corby threw it onto the bank without the net, not expecting anything but another goldeye. He glanced down the muddy river edge, his father and brother at the farthest end of the hole. He dropped the sauger into the bucket without yelling anything.

Casting out again, Corby dropped back down onto the cooler and stared into the muddy swirls. Before he was old enough to follow Sumner and their father to the big river, Corby had to stay home with his mother. Before the station wagon was out of sight she would slip a pop into his hand, pretending she was sneaking it out of the refrigerator, that they had to be careful not to get caught. Then she'd start a pan of popcorn, shaking it hard once the corn started going off, making the muscle in her arm shake. This before it was nine in the morning. Then she'd start the games—"for just the two of us"—building a fort at the foot of the bed, painting his face Indian-style with her makeup. All things she never did any other time. Corby'd seen right through it, though, and instead of playing along, he fought to stay mad, furious until the station wagon rolled back into the yard, the paddlefish huge and dead in the back, so they could see.

Now the idea that he'd ever done that to her made it hard for Corby to breathe.

The shouts, at first, seemed like something drifting in from a dream. Corby listened curiously, eyes closed, the back of his neck still tingling with the gentle touch of his mother's hand, her quiet voice urging, "Come on, Corby, won't you play with me?" Then he was able to hear his father shouting to Sumner and Corby's eyes flashed open.

Half blinded by the sudden brightness, Corby squinted in time to see his father drop his rod a long way up the bank, where it wouldn't get trampled during the fight. Free of it, he sprinted across the mud, the dried flakes tilting up beneath his boots like earthquake-broken streets.

Upstream, Sumner was standing as still as a stone, clutching his rod, line hissing off his reel, a sound so urgent Corby could hear it even from where he sat. Without wanting to, he was up and running like his father, needing to be as close as he could to whatever was happening at the other end of Sumner's line.

Corby tripped once on the way, a plate of mud giving way to the wet trapped beneath it. For a second he was skiing on the plate, then he was falling, his hands and elbows crushing through more brittle layers into the wet goo. He scrambled up and kept going.

Line was still spinning off the reel when Corby drew close, seeing that his father had hit a mud pocket himself, gumbo clinging to his knees and elbows. "Nothing to do but wait out the run," he was telling Sumner, his old voice back, quick and light. "Hardly ever see one take off like that right off the bat. Must be a real dinosaur."

Corby whispered "Ichthyosaur," but neither Sumner or his father paid any attention. Sumner's thumb was bleeding, a flap of skin hanging back where the reel handle caught him when he hit the fish in the middle of one of those wild backward rips.

"Tighten the drag a click," their father said. "He's going to have it all out soon."

Sumner kept staring at the reel, as if he'd never seen it before. It wasn't until his father began to repeat himself that he moved to follow his instructions. They started trailing the fish downstream, moving slowly, placing their steps carefully along the top of the ledge above the water.

"Go another notch," their father said.

Corby watched the line slice a tiny wake through the river, a thin stream of muddy water crawling up and dribbling back off.

"Go another."

The reel's steady whine grew labored, more growling. They walked faster downstream, pulled by the fish. Sumner said, "It's going to break."

"That rig's bombproof," their father said. "But we got to come up with some way to stop this ichthyosaur." He glanced downstream, to the end of the hole, their path blocked by willows. "Give him one more notch. Then raise your tip a second."

Sumner did as he was told. "We're into backing," he said, his voice small and sick sounding.

They were nearly running after the fish now, and when they hit a mud pocket, Sumner sliding, their father had him steadied before Corby knew he was stumbling.

When he had their feet under them again, their father said, "Come up hard with the rod."

"It's gonna break."

"Come up hard! Hit him a few times."

"The line'll break."

"Hit him! Make him hurt!"

Sumner did as he was told, tentatively at first, then bolder, angrily. Corby wasn't watching the line in the water anymore. He watched the reel, seeing the spool black and shiny between the last few twists of stringlike backing. "Almost out," he whispered.

Then the fish stopped. No slowing first. No turning. Just stopped.

The three of them staggered and their father shouted, "Reel!"

Sumner cranked and cranked, the fish allowing itself to be towed as if it had killed itself in that headlong rush. Though he was anxious to see exactly what could make a run like that, Corby suddenly didn't want to see it dead. Maybe it could still escape. He whispered, "Maybe it's just a log."

"You are so stupid!" Sumner hissed.

"He's joking, Sum'," their father said.

"Duh," Corby said, though he hadn't really been joking, just somehow wishing they could cut the line, get back to just sinking their huge hooks into nothing more than the mud shelf.

Slowly the fish began to move again, angling wearily across the river away from them, the drag tight enough that Sumner, at first, could keep reeling, only the direction of the line changing. But the fish picked up momentum and the reel handle grew stiffer and stiffer, until finally their father said, "Let him take it, Sum'."

When the fish reached the other side of the river, where their father's casts had splashed down earlier, it turned upstream, and they began to follow it again, slowly retracing the panicked steps of the first run.

For the next half hour the fish stayed on the other side of the river, first working upstream, then down, never seeming to be in a hurry, just constantly pulling them back and forth along the bank.

On one long downstream pull, they walked all the way to the cooler and Corby's rod, waving slowly up and down. "Might as well get your line in, Corb'," their father said. "If this thing ever comes across, we don't need anything for him to tangle himself in."

Corby picked up his rod, feeling the feeble run of exhausted life on the other end. "Got another one," he said.

"Probably a goldeye," Sumner answered, though he was sweating now. Corby smiled, imagining the burn in his arms.

Sumner's fish turned upstream and they followed after it, leaving Corby alone to bring in whatever it was that had managed to catch itself on his hook.

Corby reeled in quickly, flipping the exhausted fish over the mud bank. Another goldeye, hooked so deep Corby couldn't see the hook. He cut the line with his pocketknife and, looking away, dropped the fish over the bank, where it would vanish into the brown water. The monofilament slid through the eyelets, coiling around the reel.

Corby trudged upstream after Sumner and his father. When he reached them his father gave him a smile. "Wears you out, doesn't it, watching somebody work so hard?"

"Uh huh," Corby said, thinking not of Sumner, but of the fish, then of his mother.

It was another fifteen minutes before Sumner began to gain real ground. The line pointed straight across the river now, and as he continued to get it back, first in fits and starts, then more steadily, the fish began crossing to their side.

"Keep him coming," their father said, "things'll go quick now." He trotted away from them, taking the time to circle the low mud bogs, coming back with the net.

The fish was finished, Corby thought, barely resisting the incessant turning of Sumner's reel. It crossed the faint eddy line of the hole and Sumner said, "It hit the ledge. I could feel it!"

"He's beat," their father said. "Not even swimming anymore."

Sumner kept towing it in, barely walking downstream, following the drift of the fish in the current. "How close is he?" their father asked when the line pointed nearly straight up and down.

Sumner shrugged, raising his rod tip, and for a moment the water bulged, a sick grayish white expanse of back breaking clear, a tired sweep of tail. Corby whispered "Geez!" but Sumner couldn't hold it. "See it?" he asked.

Their father had seen it, but instead of answering he dodged to Sumner's other side, maneuvering the net upstream of the line. "Get ready to help with the net, Corb'," he said. "This is going to weigh a ton."

Corby stepped to his father's side, reaching for the net, but his father said, "Not until I know I've got him in. Then we'll heave him up as far as we can, just like a goldeye."

Barely turning his head toward Sumner, he said, "Can you lift him like that again?"

"I think so. Ready?"

Their father gave a quick nod and Corby watched his hands twist against the knurled aluminum net handle, the knuckles standing out white. Then he lunged. "Now, Corb'!" he grunted, and Corby grabbed for the net, seeing only its handle and his father's hands.

"Pull, Sum'!" their father shouted, and together they heaved the weight over the bank, falling after it, letting go of everything, watching the tremendous fish skid across the mud, dragging the net and rod with it.

For a moment they all lay still, breathing hard though the exertion had been only that one quick jerk. They stared at what they'd brought from the river: nearly six feet of nakedly smooth, pale, blue-gray fish, tiny sunken eyes, a bill nearly as long as the body itself, beneath which gaped a mouth like a cavern, black and bottomless, as if they'd dragged something from another age, from a hole neither light nor time had been able to reach.

Still lying down, their father whispered, "It's over a hundred easy. Maybe one twenty."

"Pounds?" Sumner asked breathlessly.

But staring at that mouth, the feeble gawping at the fatal air, the surprise in finding itself so helpless, unable to do such a simple thing as breathe, Corby could not hear their excited talk. Instead he saw again his mother's mouth, edges flecked with the whitish glue of the tape that had held down all the tubes they'd given up on. He remembered watching her mouth hang slack, wondering if she was already dead, only to have it suddenly close, her eyes suddenly open, as if the two were connected to some same string. Then her head turned to him, as if she'd known he was there all along, and she smiled slightly, lifting her hand for him to take.

She'd whispered something he hadn't been able to hear, and he'd run. Away. To get Dad, he told himself later.

Their father crept up to his knees and then to his feet, laughing though the paddlefish lay only yards away, tangled in net and line, its prehistoric mouth still working that way at the air.

"Corb'," his father said, loudly, as if he might have said it before.

He waited until Corby looked away from the fish, looked up at him.

"Run and get the knocker."

Corby glanced to Sumner, who still stared at the fish. Sumner nodded, but whispered, "Could we let him go, Dad?"

Their father closed his mouth, the smile tucked away. "No, boys. He's exhausted. He wouldn't make it now."

He eyed them both, a different, tiny smile on. "Go on, Corb'," he whispered.

Corby stood a moment more, then ran for the car, for the baseball bat—the paddlefish knocker. He used his hands in his hurry to scramble up the bank, to reach the bat, to make this end.

But once he had the bat, he stopped on the lip of the drop-off, seeing his dad and brother standing below him, one on each side of the giant fish, waiting for him.

Corby lifted the bat over his head and shouted. No words, just shouting, something, like the fish, prehistoric. When they lifted their mud-streaked faces to him, he shouted once more. Tears rolled down his cheeks and instead of sliding down to join them, he threw the bat down for them to use, then wheeled and ran from the river through the dead spring grass.

He ran as fast as he could, still shouting, hands to his ears, hoping to block the bat's last awful thwack and crunch. But what made it past his hands and his shouting was the sound of his father's steps, chasing after him. Corby pictured his father, big and fast and light again, kicking up clouds of the powder-dry gumbo, racing to bring him back.

Corby slowed, lifting his arms away from his body, waiting for the clutching grab of those white-knuckled hands, hands that would soon go loose and easy, barely hanging on, all of them back on course.

Stone

His real name is Andrew. That shortened to Andy faster than we wanted. Then, after he was old enough to do more than just plunk rocks into the water, after he'd seen me skim a few stones over the surface of a pool, he was Skipper. Marion and I didn't admire the name, it just clung to him. Fit him more than anything else.

Twelve now, on the threshold of an age I've been anxious about since before he could talk, he's told us Skipper makes him sound like a kid. He tells us he's never liked it himself. "Okay, Andrew," I answered. "No problem." But he just shook his head, told us his name now is Stone. "It's about the stone anyway, not the skipping."

I kept from rolling my eyes, but couldn't stop shooting a glance Marion's way. This is the kind of thing I've dreaded. *Stone?*

Whatever he wants to be called, he still fishes with me, which is something I am more than thankful about. Maybe I should say he *goes* fishing with me, rather than that he actually fishes. He owns a rod, but I doubt he could tell you where it is. I bought it for him years ago, an inexpensive, Kmart rig, just something to learn on. He's never used it. Oh, he carried it along the first few times, left it sitting on the cobble while he shuffled along, head down, intent as ever on his search for perfect stones, flat and smooth. Stones you could probably sell to high-powered, New Age executives, something for them to rub their fingers soothingly across, getting in touch with their inner boy.

Maybe I should have rubbed one. I still get a sick feeling remembering how I yelled at him about leaving a new rod on the rocks like that, where it would get stepped on before he knew it, broken before he'd even felt a fish through it. His face was stunned, his arms drooping limp to his sides, stilled by my roar; a black beauty of a stone suddenly nothing but a dead weight caught in the curl of his finger and thumb.

Without saying a word he walked back to the rod and carried it with him the rest of the afternoon, tip high as he poked through the stones, carrying them one at a time down to the edge of the river. There he'd twist and fire, the rock skipping and skipping, finally easing into the water as gently as a returned trout. It was plain how the rod threw off his balance, the usual perfect grace of his motion. This when he wasn't more than seven. Almost half his life ago. I didn't make him bring the rod again.

Not that I forced him into any of this. He always asked to go. The few times I left him behind I was nearly afraid to return home, to face his silent reproach, his gaping disappointment. But he wasn't somebody I could bring when there were serious fishermen along. I mean, all he ever did was throw stones. Into the water. Even my best friends would have had a hard time putting up with that.

So over the years, my fishing has changed to adapt to my son. My whole life paring away to only him. He is my sole partner now, and he does not fish. He never once made a cast with that rod. When he was really small, less than two, he used to get tired, worn out from lugging boulders out of the ground and thumping them down in the shallows. Then he'd make me sit and he'd crawl into my lap. I'd place his hands on the rod, letting him follow the motion of the cast, flicking out tiny ten-footers, fifteen, floating a Renegade or something as easy through a drift of five or six feet.

We once caught a rainbow doing that. Nothing more than six inches, closer in than the run I'd been fishing, too young to be spooked down by cast after cast over its head. I'd gotten all excited, whispering, "You got him, Andy! You got him!"

Andy had grinned, exactly the same way he did when I caught a fish on my own. I ran the line between his fingers, let him feel the run and tug of the little trout, but he only held it, not hauling in, not even jerking back, unsurprised by the life in the line.

When I brought the trout into the shallows, where Andy could see him, he clambered off my lap, trudging right into the water, the river seeping into his sneakers, his socks. He squatted before the fish, soaking his pants and diaper. He simply gazed at the trout, same as ever, mesmerized by its fluid motion, even as it sat quiet, holding against whatever tiny current there was, mouth opening and closing against the bite of fly. He never reached to touch them, never shouted or hooted, or wanted to keep one. They held him like a house fire holds some adults, blankly in awe.

When I released a fish, he'd watch until it darted from sight. Then, the spell broken, he'd smile up at me for a moment, and return to shore, beginning the search for the next perfect stone.

He could curl his body like a whip, a spring coiled around the stone locked between his thumb and finger. When he let loose, spinning and firing, his arm and hand arced out only inches above the water. I would sometimes forget my own fishing, sometimes drown and drag a fly as I counted skips, as I watched the stone unwind, the skips slower, closer together, until finally the stone shimmered across the top, leaving a wake, settling down to vanish.

When he was smaller, learning to count, I'd yell out the totals, "One! Two! Three! Four! Five!"—hardly ever less than that—"Six! Seven! Eight!" until I was finally counting so fast the numbers blurred. He wouldn't look at me, but he couldn't hide his smile. He'd straighten out of his skipper's crouch and turn away from the river, head down, already consumed by the next throw. This when most kids couldn't throw ten feet.

We developed a strategy, me fishing only the head of every pool, leaving the broad, quiet bodies for him. Sometimes, if stones were scarce, hard to find, I'd take a quick few casts for the big, deep fish. Now and then I'd catch him waiting, the first stone already in place, but standing back, letting me finish. Even then, though, even as he waited and watched, it was the water he watched, not me. He studied eddy lines and swirls, chop and break, anything that might upset the flight of his stone. Not holding water, not cover, not feeding lanes.

At least once or twice a year, I'd ask if he'd like to give it a try, holding out my rod, only half an arm's length out. He'd purse his lips, tilt his head, as if giving it serious consideration. But always he'd begin flicking his wrist, a stone in place, and shake his head. "I don't think so," he'd say. "I think I've got myself a good one here."

And I'd nod back, clack over the stones to my place at the head of the pool, where the water ran quick to join the deep run. Watching his throws from the corner of my eye.

Baseball, I'd think. If I could ever divert that single-minded passion to a pitching mound and a backstop, he'd be in the majors before he finished junior high. But grass and diamonds, all that dry-land stuff, left him cold. I bought mitts (had them bought before he was born, to tell the truth, all that father-son stuff a myth I'd dreamed of for years). We'd play catch sometimes in the street, but his face was not the same, his body hardly in the game. On the street or lawn his throws were jerky, graceless things; only humoring my parental fantasies, playing ball with the old man.

But on the river it was pure. It was not something he did for me or anyone else. Even for himself, I sometimes thought. It was more as if the river pulled it out of him, wrapping him around those stones the way the river flowed around a boulder: like quicksilver, easy and relentless.

He's always been quiet, keeping his own counsel, and though we've wondered about that, even worried about it sometimes, he seems like a good kid, thoughtful. Not crazy. Not dangerous. Not lurking with moods. So the other day, only a week after announcing his name was Stone, when he came back late from school with his hair—I don't know, braided I guess, dozens of braids, little blond pickaninny things sticking up every which way, furrows shaved down to bone in between—Marion and I could only stare.

"Lovely," I finally managed to stammer, and we sat down and ate.

The next evening, though the weather was threatening, I walked into the living room where he sat reading the paper. The front page. A twelve-year-old. Only the tops of his tassels were visible above the screen of newsprint. This was the kind of thing the mere idea of had given me goose bumps for a decade.

"I'm heading up Belt Creek," I said. "Want to go?"

I braced myself for the first-ever rejection, the first in what would be a hopeless, endless string, but the paper dropped to the table and he stretched up from the couch, already nearly as tall as me. "Sure," he said.

We didn't speak on the short drive. I glanced between the road, the clouds, and the river, catching quick glimpses of the tremulous braids, quivering in the motion of the car.

At the river he waited for me to wader up, to settle on an Adams and tie it on. Then he slipped down through the willow leaves, his basketball shoes huge and untied on his feet.

We'd worked this hole many times, one of the biggest pools on the creek. A skipper's mecca. By the time I broke through the willows, he was already turning over the first stone, studying, then rejecting. There was a chance I could get one drift the length of the pool while he searched, but I stood just at the outside edge of the branches and watched.

It wasn't until he settled on a stone, already into his weighing, judging wrist flicks, that he noticed me still behind him, not up at the head of the run. He raised an eyebrow, waiting for an explanation.

I could barely look at him, his head like a museum diorama of some war-ravaged cornfield. I glanced around him, up the hole and down.

"You want to take a cast or two first?" he asked.

I stared at him. It wasn't a question he'd ever asked before. We had a system. We knew our roles.

I shook my head. Stretching out my arm, holding the rod toward him, I asked, "You?"

He grinned, tossing the rock in his hand. "I don't think so," he answered. "I think I've got myself a good one here."

I nodded, but couldn't stop myself. "Why don't you, Stone?" I said, stumbling a little on the new name, holding the rod out as far as I could. "At least give it a try."

He looked at me as blankly as I must have looked at him. His smile was gone.

Maybe, I hoped, he was just getting set for his throw, working up his game face. But I thought it more likely I'd blundered across some line I should have seen.

I shrugged, waving him toward the river. "Go ahead," I said, my voice only a croak. "I want to watch."

And that fast I stood hollowed on the edge of the willow break, the river running before us, wondering what it would be like to be able to really fish again, to work the long deep runs with double nymphs, to start low and work my way up, leaving no flash of water untested. To fish the way I had before he was born: serious, determined, concentrating the same way he did with his stones, cleaned out and fresh by the time I began the drive back home to Marion. Alone. There was nothing I could imagine that would be emptier.

Just before the river's edge, he paused. Without turning to look at me he said, "You going to count?"

I nearly took a step back. He'd never asked that, and I wondered if he could really remember back that far, when he couldn't have been more than four years old. Maybe five.

"No," I answered. "I'll just watch."

He shrugged and then his face was only his game face. He stepped to the edge of the running water, ground his sneaker into the rock until he was satisfied. Then he took a breath, coiled in upon himself, and, before my eye could really catch it, he let go.

I didn't watch the stone. I watched him; his braids whipping along with his arm, the vast power whirling through him: leg, hip, shoulder, elbow, wrist. His set foot pulled free in the follow-through, splashing down in the river, his legs spread wide, just like a pitcher falling off the mound. His face, still turned away from me, followed the path of his stone.

I heard the sharp strike of the stone against the cliff face across the creek, and I closed my eyes, trying to hold him there forever.

I thought it was only for a second, but then I felt the tug on my rod. Startled, I stepped back, opened my eyes to see Andy, Skipper, Stone, whoever, pulling my fly rod away from me.

"Okay," he snapped. "If you think it's so important."

"What? I . . ." But I stopped.

He was already heading back to the river, already flicking the rod tip, working out line for a cast. I took a step after him. "Stone," I said.

He shook his head, again not looking at me, again nothing but concentration. It began to rain, a steady, cold drizzle I doubt he noticed.

Once he worked the line out, he settled into casting. Not fishing. Casting. He worked the line the way he threw, putting his shoulders into it, his legs. The line essed out and back, out and back, great, silent yellow arcs against the low gray of the sky. As far as I knew, the only thing he knew about casting was from watching me, which could only have been a glimpse here and there, stolen from his search for the stones.

But now he was casting as far as I could, farther, still without a thought of letting the fly down, of where or how to put it over a trout. "Stone?" I said.

And then I heard the tiny crack. For an instant I smiled, thinking he'd overreached himself, that he'd snapped the fly off on a badly timed cast. That there were still things he needed me to teach him. But then I realized what he'd done. He'd cast and cast until he reached the cliff, the Adams striking the limestone wall the same way his perfect stone had.

And as soon as he'd done that, he was through. My fly line drifted limp in the rain-pocked river, the current carrying it away in helpless, slack loops. I watched it go, still numb from watching him cast.

"Okay," he said. I heard his breath coming hard and fast. I'd never seen anyone cast that way.

"Okay," he said again. "Now you throw one of mine." He bent down, searching for another perfect stone. He held my rod tip high, that lesson never forgotten.

I cleared my throat. "I couldn't, Stone. I'm forty years old. I'd be on the chiro's table for a week if I tried one of your throws."

He straightened, eyeing me, turning a stone blindly in his fingers. The rain had slicked his hair, the braids matted down over the shaven furrows, a new degree of awfulness.

"Forty's not so old," he said, suddenly spinning the stone at me with a nasty, quick backhand. I snagged it, clamping it between both hands just before it struck my chest.

"Come on," he said. "Before this rain washes away my braids."

79

I curled my thumb and forefinger around the stone, feeling its heft, its smoothness. It could all be washed away. I tried to remember every trace of Andy's motion, tried to picture myself making the same moves, the same way he must have pictured me casting.

"I think you got yourself a good one there," he prompted. "I think you should be able to make it across."

I stepped to the edge of the river, and dug in my foot the way he had. I coiled inward, pent-up energy. "I don't want to make it across," I whispered.

Then, picturing a last time that cast of his, all those stones, I let go.

Grayfish

Eating through the crusted layer of old snow, the fire smudged the dingy edges of its own hole with black. The pine Marty and John threw on was heavy with resin and pitchy smoke swept upward. They threw on more and more wood, because they were wet and cold and there was no end to the wood. Soon tongues of flame shot up taller than either of them. They laughed at the wildness, then fell quiet, staring into the fire's glowing heart.

A long, twisted sheet of birch bark at the edge of the fire, where the snow had been shortly before, began to writhe, and the men watched it curl tighter and tighter and then begin to unfold again. Its inside, the side that had wrapped the tender parts of the tree, ignited and the white bark on the outside began to brown. Marty said it looked like a marshmallow, ready to come out. But then an old weakness, a knothole maybe, gave way, and a mouth opened in the bark and widened, stretching as if in some awful, silent shriek. Fire belched forth. The bark was engulfed then and hard to see and Marty didn't say anything else for some time.

Steam began to rise from their pants and they turned around and stood letting their rears toast. Marty said they should be on spits. He looked over at John and John looked back and smiled. Talking was a habit with Marty—was with most people. Even up here alone with his brother he kept at it. Some habits were harder to break than others, and Marty figured it didn't hurt anything.

When the last batch of wood began to truly burn it was too hot to stand near the fire and they shuffled down the brief strip of broken rock to the lake's shoreline. Just beyond the edge of thin, fragile ice, the young grayling patrolled, their big fins down, their blue spots muted by the sky's gray.

This wasn't Alaska, not true grayling country, but down in the lower states, the last remnants of a forgotten stocking effort. The lake itself was high and out of the way. The fish had reproduced unchecked, until they choked the lake with this ring of marauding dwarfs. But bigger fish were out there. The record in this state was something over seventeen inches, and they caught several larger than that every year. Especially in the spring, if they caught the ice-out right. But if they'd turned in the records they'd have had to say where they were caught. Marty could get John worked into a silent furor just teasing about turning one of the monsters in for a record.

This morning, after the long, soggy hike through snow still deep in the draws, and after the long wondering if the lake was open yet, they had crested the last ridge and seen the sheen of open water. With that driving away the cold, they'd set up their rods and gone after them, same as every year, content to slaughter the smaller fish, thinking there was

something the two of them could do in the way of popula-
tion control.

Just as the cold was returning, though, nagging for the
fire, Marty had reared back and launched his longest cast.
John had been working shorter and shorter, rather than
pushing the ice out of his guides. Marty felt him watching,
timing the drop of the weighted nymph. He began the hop-
ping retrieve exactly when John would've, and grinned when
John gave his low, grunting whoop of approval, shaking his
fist at him. Then the fish hit, and as soon as John saw how
the rod bowed he came barreling down the beach to see if
he could help.

But the grayling gave up easily, as they did now and then,
and by the time John was there Marty had it sidling in, first
running right, then wearily left. Its ridiculous, gorgeous fin
was spread wide, fighting the pull, and the blood surge of
the fight brightened its red and blue spots as if the fish itself
were alight.

Marty had to break a channel through the shore ice with
his boot, then, when he eased the fish from the water, they
held it against John's rod. Marty flattened the tail, aligning it
with the cork butt. The fish's small, jutting mouth reached
about an inch past the nick that marked the state record, but
stopped just short of John's personal nick—his personal
world record. A quarter inch short.

John gave another of his deep, whooping roars and
slapped Marty on the back. Marty bent over the water again,
hands in the icy lake, reviving the strangely fragile fish.
John's last rough slap nearly tipped him over, and he let go
of the fish to stop his fall. The fish darted down the steep
drop into the black heart of the lake, as if it had only feigned
weakness. Marty was laughing by then, too, and he realized

John had kept up his demented whooping. It echoed back from the rock and snow and timber, surrounding them.

The old mark on the rod, the longest one, was ten years old now, a fluke, Marty always said. But John held by it, and each fish that missed only pleased him more. For years Marty had wanted to see one of his fish's rubbery lips eclipse that mark, but they had always fallen just that much short.

After Marty released the fish, they'd moved up the shoreline and started the fire. Always before they had simply built a small warming fire, but John was still wound up about the big fish, and he had been the one to go farther into the trees, bringing back the logs. Soon they were trying to outdo each other, until the fire took on a life of its own, driving them back to the water.

They chipped the ice from the line guides and started around the lake to the willow thicket at the outlet. John slipped on the ice once, going all the way down, twisting to land on his rear, holding his rod high, away from danger. Marty turned to see if he was all right and John was smiling hard, pulling himself up. Then Marty started to laugh, pointing, and finally pulling on John's beard, the tip of which was curled and shortened from the heat of the fire. "You burned your beard!" he said, laughing.

John didn't understand, and Marty tugged harder on his beard, pulling it around for John to see. John winced and slapped Marty's arm away. Marty went through the necessary pantomime then, and John's face lit up and he began tugging at his beard himself, feeling the thick, coarse patch of burned hair. He laughed, and Marty wondered how it was that laughing was the only normal sound he could make. It was fitting—he was always laughing—but still Marty wondered. He knew he was the only one who ever heard the wild, excited shouting. Their parents had convinced John early on that the shouting scared people, but out in the mountains, even as kids, Marty had worked against that training, until John had begun to shout simply for the reaction it caused in his brother. At least that's what Marty figured. Deaf as a stone from birth, John had no other reason to shout that Marty could see.

The pantomime reminded Marty of the first time up here, finding the lake without knowing what lay beneath its surface. The little grayling were ferocious, and John landed the first while Marty was still setting up his rod. He'd carried it over, the question look on his face.

Marty had just returned from Alaska, where he'd been working on a crab boat, which, he would say later, was proof of just how young and dumb a person could be. The grayling surprised him, but he knew they had stocked everything up here at one time or another. But his mind had drawn a blank on the name. Gray something, gray something. John shook the fish under his nose, wanting an identification.

Marty had squatted then, writing "Gray" in the sand with his finger. Then he pounded his fist against the shore, looking up at John and shaking his head. John squatted beside him just as Marty wrote "Grayfish." He knew that wasn't right. He was thinking out loud.

John's hand had swept across the sand, obliterating the word. His laughter pealed across the lake. First he wrote "Moron," with an arrow pointing to Marty. Marty laughed a little but, though he'd been away for a year, he still recalled all the times he'd heard kids shouting that word, and he did not look at John. The next word John wrote was "Grayling."

Marty laughed. "That's it. I knew that."

Later, when Marty was working shrimp on the Texas gulf, John had sent him a cutout of a grayling, on gray construction paper. On the back side was written "Grayfish (*Fishus grayus*)." There was nothing else in the envelope and Marty had laughed until he nearly cried.

Now they walked toward the willows again, more carefully on the ice, because Grayfish really was a place far enough away, and high enough up, that even a sprain could mean bad things.

Marty parted the first of the branches and the raft was still there. They dragged it out together, sweating before they were through, although the logs seemed dry and buoyant once they edged them into the lake. Ten years ago they'd brought up the rope and lashed the dead lodgepoles together, pushing the platform out into the lake, wondering if they were just going for a quick swim. They hadn't even had the paddles then, and Marty doubted there was ever a less stable craft built. But they'd eased it past the band of stunted fish, out into deeper and deeper water, where there was no bottom, where the big fish rose. That was when the record-breakers really began to fall.

Since then the raft had been modified. One year an outrigger had been added, and the next, in the greatest innovation, they'd dumped the outrigger in favor of a double raft, a kind of catamaran, with a raised floor of thin pine poles. It still steered like a bathtub, but it kept them more or less out of the water, and they could both cast at once, if they were careful.

And they were always careful. Today, Marty knew, with the low, heavy layer of cloud and the ice girdling the lake, a dump in deep water might be the end of things, even before shore, and the fire, could be reached. He'd seen a young hand go over the side of a crabber off the Aleutians. He'd been blue and stiff before he could be retrieved and he never did make it back.

Marty grabbed John's arm and pointed at the ice and the clouds and the water. He made the *careful* sign then, and John nodded and they pushed off, digging the frayed ends of their canoe paddles against the frozen sand ripples on the bottom until their raft was free.

There was nothing fancy involved. They simply paddled straight out until the bottom was gone and then a little farther. Maybe one hundred yards. They'd explored the lake before and the raft was beached off the most productive spot, though it had been a toss-up, one place seemingly as good as the next.

They started stripping line out together and John saw the first rise, off to the left, followed a moment later by a second, coming closer. Neither one of them could see what the fish might be rising to, but these were the least-particular fish they'd ever known. They left on their small Hare's Ears, and John dropped his past and in front of the path of rises.

He hooked up immediately and the fish did not give up as Marty's had. John was as silent as ever while the fight was on, and Marty, guessing the fish would be close to that final nick, watched John's eyes, quick and alert where they followed the cut of the line through the flat, steely surface of the lake. He grinned again at the singed beard, the flaps of the woolen cap dangling foolishly over the useless ears.

Marty took his net from over his shoulder but John waved him away. He netted the fish himself, swiftly, before it was worn down. He held his rod to the water and gave a quiet grunt and released the grayling without lifting it from the lake. He smiled then, looking at Marty and holding his thumb and finger a half inch apart. That much short. His fingertips were red where they poked through the sodden wool of his gloves. He wouldn't even show Marty the fish unless it broke at least the state record.

The raft circled slowly in a breeze that hardly marred the stillness of the lake. Marty caught a fish the size of the young marauders and he held it up, shouting at it, asking what the hell it was doing out in the deep. His words, and John's laughing, echoed across the lake again. He killed the fish to add to the stringer they would have for dinner and wedged it into a crack between the decking logs.

The cloud cover eased down while they fished, until the mountains disappeared, the trees rising up their flanks blending into a foggy gray-green. The lake turned even darker, nearly black, smooth as a slate. Tiny globes of the mist beaded onto the hairs of their clothing until they glistened. Anywhere they touched broke the beads and the cloth turned dark and wet before more mist pearled up.

Even the breeze died as the lake socked in and the raft stopped its slow twist. It left Marty facing the shore, where the fire still burned steadily. As he watched, a pulsing red ring formed around the fire, flaring out, falling back, and surging forth again, a trick of flame and moisture. Marty stared at it, forgetting to fish, and when he reached across their frail raft and tugged on John's arm he didn't know that John was bringing in a fish.

He turned when John jerked his arm away, and then tugged again. John looked over his shoulder, annoyed, but when he saw the fire and its ring the scowl dropped away from his face and he sat and stared. The awed smile stole so slowly over his features that Marty didn't see it form. Then the ring wavered and winked out. Although they looked for a minute or two more, the halo did not return.

Then John was tugging at Marty's arm, holding up another grayling, and his fingers again, showing it was just shy of the all-time world record. Marty smiled slowly, then waved his hand, dismissing the fish. He slapped himself on the chest, saying his was much bigger than that, and John laughed and let the fish go. Marty listened to the laugh, a pulsing glory around his brother, and stripped line for another cast.

The fishing out deep was slower than the frantic hookings of the small fish near shore, but the fish were all big, except for the midget Marty'd killed. It was near dusk, and they were both wet from the mist, and the fire had settled down to little more than a glow. They'd each landed several fish near record size, but none as close as Marty had come from shore. Marty tapped John and pointed at his wrist and the fire and nodded his head toward shore.

John agreed and held up a finger in the traditional last-cast sign. This was the contest of them all and Marty stripped out all the line he could possibly cast, giving himself that much more chance. He'd always been able to cast farther than his brother and when their lines touched down he made faces at John, showing him what he thought of such a tiny cast. John smiled back, giving him the finger.

John hooked up first, a big fish, and he started his war whoop for the first time since Marty had landed the fish from shore. He fought carefully but never looked away from Marty, his face lit up, taunting him. He whooped again and the dew shook away from his beard.

It really was an ugly noise, that whoop, and Marty knew his parents were right. It would scare people. But he laughed back at his brother and turned to his own line. He'd let it sink too deep and when he jigged his rod tip the strike was so solid he thought he might have embedded the nymph in some ancient drowned tree. But then his line was off and running and in the moment when he still had time he lunged across the raft to slap John, to show him what he had. He saw John's face, stunned and not smiling for an instant before he heard the whooping blurt out again and again, as if the lid had been jarred loose from some torment long buried.

The fish turned before Marty tightened up, then quartered, keeping the line taut, testing its pull. Then it broke away again, ticking line off the reel. By the cut of the line Marty knew the fish was changing depths, coming up, seeing if that would free itself. Marty wondered how long it'd been since the fish had left the murky depths he'd let his fly sink to.

The fish didn't break the surface before it turned again, coming in on Marty, and he stripped line back. He'd never seen anything but grayling come from this lake, but this fish fought with an experience and power that he'd never before felt in any grayling.

It was still down deep when it went under the raft, on John's side. Marty leaped that way, passing his rod to John, who gave a startled grunt as the raft tipped crazily down. He took the rod from Marty, passing it under his, which was still bucking with his fish. John's eyes went wide in the moment he touched the rod, and he gave it back to Marty, his mouth slack, grinning.

Marty crab-crawled back to his side of the raft and the fish seemed to just give up. It was holding sideways again, like the fish in the morning—the famous grayling trick of spreading its prehistoric fin, making the fisherman drag it through the water if he could. He glanced at John, wondering what he could have transmitted through the rod to this fish to make it give in so easily.

John was netting his fish. Marty saw the rod go down, and he saw the smile again. Then Marty glanced back to his line, its yellow curve having a little belly back in it as the fish came in with less and less resistance.

Then just beyond the end of the yellow stripe in the black water, the fish appeared, still holding sideways, every fin flared as wide as possible, the bright shocks of color burning through the darkness of the lake. The body, bowed away from the pull, was long and broad, a gargantuan unlike any they had ever pulled from the lake.

It shook once, weakly, and just at the edge of his vision Marty could see John with his fish out of the water, pinned against the deck, measuring it against his rod. He saw the intensity in his brother's face, the precision of the judging, and, still holding the fish down, John lifted his head back, eyes closed, and howled out his whoops.

Marty tore back on his rod. He saw the fish jerk through the water and fight again, pulling away, and Marty ripped back once more. He felt the tippet part and saw the fish start backward then stop, hanging motionless for an instant before its own muscles took over and it was gone with one flash of color.

Marty didn't take the time to stare after it. Instead he slammed his rod down and began to swear. But he wasn't listening to himself. He was listening to that frightening cry, rebounding through the lake's cirque, ringing them in their ridiculous, dangerous raft as surely as the ghostly corona had ringed the fire.

He turned then to John, who had just seen that Marty had lost the fish and was laughing too hard to keep whooping.

He pointed at his fish, and Marty crawled carefully to where John had it pinned against the rod, its lip just touching their world-record mark.

Marty shook his head as if he was disappointed and pointed at the water where his fish had disappeared. He held his hands up, a good two feet apart, and John had tears running from his eyes, down to his singed beard, and he nodded his head vigorously, shaking his finger at the same spot in the water, his mouth gaping with laughter. Marty could hear the scream inside his brother's head, "That's right! That's right! That's exactly where your fish is! In the lake!"

Marty waved his brother's laughing away and picked up his paddle, starting for shore while John revived his fish and released it to the lake. But it was hopeless without John paddling to balance his effort and Marty stopped.

He watched his brother's back hunched over the black water, the dew still glistening off his coat. He'd broken the fish off out of pity, and Marty hated himself for that. John had never pitied himself a day in his life. Marty'd once, a long time ago, told John that he would give him his ears, if he could. It was a stupid, useless thing to say, and John had just smiled and written, "Who'd want those car doors?"

John straightened on his side of the raft after the fish had stirred and shot away, and Marty swatted him with his paddle, pointing to shore. He turned forward then, away from his brother, but he thought he could still hear the dying quaver of John's victory cry, rippling through the cirque like a haunting.

My Sister's Hood

The dim hands of the clock finally crawled past four-thirty. By four-thirty-one I knew Allen had only been showing off. All his talk of his fishing boat, of the days and days it took to score on a muskie—*but when you do, holy man!*—hadn't been anything more than scoring points with my sister.

But then, in the distance, I picked up the throaty rumble of his car—the one that made my dad grumble "Hood!" every time he took Alice away. I always smiled when Dad said that. I mean, how many hoods have muskie boats on Long Lake?

Already dressed, I flung back my covers, stepped into my tennis shoes, and leaped downstairs. I'd tie them in the car.

Snagging my fishing rod and tackle box, the bag lunch Mom had left for me, I blew through the front door. I tore down the walk to Allen's idling car, his headlights flashing off the garbage cans, bright against the white garage door.

From the backseat someone laughed and said, "What? You been waiting up all night?"

I skidded to a stop beside Allen's door, my mouth suddenly bone dry. There was only supposed to be me and Allen.

"Hey, Frank," Allen said, lounging his arm out his window. "Slip your rod in there with the rest of them."

I did as I was told, threading my rod through the half-open rear window, fighting to keep the reel handle from touching any of the other rods, the grabbing eyelets. The car was full, three other guys besides Allen. Probably all seniors. I was in third grade. At least he hadn't called me Franky, the way Alice still did.

I didn't notice Allen until he tugged at the tackle box in my hand. "We'll put this stuff in the trunk," he said. "We're pretty cramped up front. Didn't know these clowns'd be coming."

Setting my tackle box on top of the spare tire, I cleared my throat. "You don't have to take me," I whispered. It was the first time I'd ever volunteered not to go fishing.

"Naw," Allen said. He was at his door already, waiting for me to climb into the middle, straddling the hump, the gear shift. "We got room."

I slid into my place and when Allen scrunched in beside me, I whispered, "I brought worms. They're in with my lunch," trying to show I wouldn't be a problem. But the same guy who'd asked if I'd stayed up all night said, "You brought worms for lunch? Wow. Trade you for my Milky Way."

Allen glanced over his shoulder, but I could see his smile in the light reflecting off the garage door. "You guys," he said, "this is Frank." He looked at each of them, rattling off names I forgot before he stopped talking.

"Frank's a fishing fool," Allen said. Then he added, "Frank is Alice's little brother, too," making it sound like a threat, and I slumped in my seat, my butt vibrating as soon as Allen touched the gas.

He squealed the tires backing out of the drive, and again in the street, starting off. I bit back my smile, thinking of Dad in bed, grumbling, "What does she see in that hood?"

After the introduction it was like I wasn't there. Allen turned up the radio, and pretty soon they were shouting over it. I tried listening: complaints about some teacher; something that happened on the way home from the last football game. But it was like listening to my parents and their friends, and pretty soon I just listened to the radio. It was on the same station I heard thumping through the wall of Alice's bedroom.

Then the guy who'd teased me about the worms tapped my shoulder, shouting, "What do you say, Frank? Give us the scoop."

"What?" I asked, leaning away from him.

"About Alice."

I looked at the glowing light of the radio. "What?"

"Tell us," he said, laughing a little. "About Alice."

"What about her?" My voice squeaked.

Allen growled, "Towers," and I almost looked for something reaching into the sky before realizing Towers was his name.

"What's she say about Al?" Towers asked, ignoring Allen. "She hot for him?"

I tried to keep my eyes from going wide. Allen said, "Towers, you want to walk home? I told you, this is Alice's little brother."

"What do you think I'm asking him for?" he answered, still laughing, but I could hear the rattle of the rods as he sat back. He didn't ask again.

I sat dazed, thinking of Alice hot for anyone. Anyone hot for Alice. My sister. My leg was practically touching Allen's, and I pinched it tight against the stick shift. I wondered if Alice rode next to him like this, in the middle.

They were talking again, but I was too stunned to hear. Until someone whistled and said "Tits like torpedoes" and I knew they couldn't be talking about Alice anymore.

The guy beside me laughed and said, "How the hell would you know, Krankill?"

"Oh, I know, Lindy," he answered back, with a big wavery sigh. "Big *silky* torpedoes." He paused and even over the radio I could hear them breathing. "Oh, yes," Krankill added, sounding like he was licking his chops. "Armed and dangerous."

Allen laughed this time, saying, "I'll tell you what's dangerous: You guys allowed out without your brains."

"Oh, I got brains all right," Krankill said from the back. He rustled around. "Let me unzip here and I'll show you just how big my brain is."

He pretended to open his fly and the car was filled with laughing and catcalls, Towers screaming, "Even a *fly* couldn't think with something that small!"

Suddenly I was flattened against the dash, the brakes screeching, the stick shift rammed into my leg, way too close to my own privates. Then we were stopped and Allen was screaming, "He's *Alice's little brother!*"

The laughter gave out slowly, somebody snickering a second after everything went quiet.

"All right?" Allen said. "You guys got that?"

"Got it," somebody said, fast and stupid sounding.

Allen put the car in gear, pushing the stick away from my crotch, but his hand stayed there on the knob, hovering, making me sweat.

Before he stepped on the gas Allen said, "Now knock it off. You want Alice hearing about all you running around with your dipsticks dangling out?"

"Only if she'll show me a place to dip it," Towers said.

Allen spun around so fast Towers was blurting, "Just kidding, Al. Just goofing off. Sorry," before I'd quite heard what he said.

Allen sat back down, laying a long patch this time, the squeal of tires stretching out and out, angrier every second. But he shifted at last and then we were just flying down the path of his headlights, only driving toward the lake again.

I whispered, "I'd never tell Alice. Not anything."

Allen nodded, so small a move I barely saw it, but from the back Towers said, "'At a boy, kid."

After that no one said another word until we pulled onto the last bit of gravel to the lake. The sky was lighter now, the trees hiding the lake black against it, and when we cut through the gap in the woods the lake shone the same metal color as the sky, just the way I'd known it would, though I'd never been anywhere near here. There was only one boat cutting the flat water. Maybe two.

With all that water out there I could hardly sit still, but Allen parked at the end of the dock and everybody crawled out slowly, stretching and yawning while I waited.

Towers crawled out with all the fishing rods and started down the dock, stumbling at first, not used to the pitch and sway of the narrow planks. I carried down my own tackle box and lunch bag, plus another tackle box, twice the size of mine. I followed Towers to the slot in the dock and looked down at the tiny boat there—just an old aluminum rowboat with nothing but a tiny, oil-stained trolling motor bolted onto a broken sliver of plywood.

Towers dumped the rods down in front, but I held onto my stuff. I looked again at the boat, thinking Towers must not even know where to go.

Back on shore Allen and Lindy were talking to each other. They stepped aside as Krankill staggered past, lugging an enormous metal cooler. He dropped it between the rowboat seats with a gonging bang that they could've heard back home.

I looked again at the boat, already cramped with the rods and cooler. Krankill took the huge tackle box from my hand. "Thanks, man," he said, and dropped that in beside the rods, the plastic box nearly as loud as the cooler.

There was no way we were all going to fit in that boat. I saw already how I'd get left on the dock with my worms, fishing for perch, just like I did whenever I talked anyone into taking me fishing, taking me close enough to any water I could try. I'd never fished from a boat in my life, just watched from shore, wishing.

I saw how the ride back would go, Allen getting nice, working it so I wouldn't tell Alice they'd just dumped me here. Picked me up so she'd think they were being nice to me, then got rid of me. Drive me home at the end of the day, make me promise not to tell, like I already had promised. Like an idiot.

Allen and Krankill came down the dock together carrying another tackle box and a minnow bucket. I bent down to tie my shoes, just catching Allen cracking his first big, ingratiating smile at me. "What do you think, Franky?"

Franky. I shrugged, thinking, *You call this tub a fishing boat? I'd be embarrassed to be seen bailing it. I wouldn't be caught . . .*

"I'm saving up for a real outboard," Allen said. "We'll be zooming to the hot spots then."

I nodded, tugging my laces tight, waiting for the ax to fall. Lindy dropped the last cooler in, and we all stood on the dock. "Gonna be cramped," Lindy said, like he'd rehearsed.

"You mind sitting on the cooler up front?" Allen asked me.

I shook my head.

"Then Lindy and Kranky'll sit across the middle. I'll take the back, run the power plant."

Towers looked around. "What . . ."

"Sorry, Towers. Not enough room."

Towers grunted out a laugh. "Yeah," he said. "Right."

Krankill and Lindy stepped in, rocking everything, and Allen untied the lines, tossing them into the boat. "Go on, Frank," he said, waving me forward. "Hop in."

"Hey," Towers said, lifting his leg to step over the edge of the boat.

Allen grabbed my arm, lifting me into the boat. I tried not to step on any of the rods.

"Look, Towers," Allen said, holding up a hand to keep him out of the boat, "if the kid's interested, maybe you can still trade him for his worms. Catch yourself a mess of perch." He bent over quick, picking a rod out of the tangle and tossing it to Towers like a baseball bat.

Towers caught it, one foot still lifted off the dock.

"Or," Allen said, wrapping a cord around the top of the motor, "if you don't feel like fishing, maybe you can find someplace to dip your stick." He gave the cord a pull and the engine coughed. He wrapped and pulled again. The motor caught, puffing a little blue cloud.

Towers still stood clutching his fishing rod, both his feet down flat on the dock now.

I uncrinkled the top of my lunch bag and took out my worms, but Lindy touched my hand. "You don't have to give him those."

Allen backed out of the slot.

"What about my lunch?" Towers shouted, though we were still only a few feet away.

"Kranky," Allen said, and Krankill opened the cooler. He flung a sandwich at Towers.

It started unwrapping in midair, but only a piece of lettuce fluttered out when it hit Towers's chest. He pinched the sandwich there, against his fishing rod. "This is total bull-shit," Towers said. "Riding all the way up here. . . ."

I put my head down, studying the inside of my lunch bag.

Krankill laughed behind me and reached into the cooler again. "Hey, Towers," he said, "catch!" He winged an apple that Towers let sail over his head. It splashed down next to a real fishing boat, bobbing there.

"Assholes!" Towers shouted.

Krankill threw a can of something at him that didn't quite reach. Everybody in the boat but me chuckled. The tiny out-board throbbed, driving us away from the dock about as fast as you could walk, if you could walk out here, on the water. Towers kept shouting "Assholes!" growing fainter.

Then, when we were nearly too far to hear, he stopped. Instead he must've taken a huge breath, because his next shout rang over the water clear as a bell, "I'll tell you what, Al, hell'd freeze over before I'd ever dip my stick anywhere near where you've been!"

Allen threw the steering stick to the side so hard the boat shuddered. Sitting high on my cooler I had to grab its han-dles to keep from going overboard. We began lumbering through a huge, arcing curve, but Towers was already running up the dock, hitting shore and still going, back up the road through the slot in the trees.

"Prick," Allen said, straightening the boat back out the way we'd been going.

"Think he'll get a ride?" Lindy asked.

"Who cares?"

"What a prick," Allen said again, and for a minute nobody said anything else. Then Allen said, "Don't pay any attention to him, Frank."

I nodded, thinking of Alice and Allen. Even if it were true, Alice doing something like that, it was too gross to even think about Towers knowing about it—him being able to picture her that way. I wished they'd left me on the dock instead of Towers. I wished I'd never come.

Then, after a few minutes more, Allen cut the motor and said, "Well, kid, ready to try for one of these muskies?"

I nodded, doubting now that any of these guys really knew how to fish for such a legend, no matter what Allen said when he hung out with me, waiting for Alice.

"Okay," he said. "You ever hook a minnow?"

"Practically," I said with a tiny laugh, thinking of some of the puny bluegills I'd caught from shore.

"Not catch," Allen said, laughing. "I mean, for bait."

I blushed and shook my head. But Allen only said, "Show him, Lindy."

The minnow Lindy snagged from the bucket wasn't a minnow, it was practically a keeper. "Shiner," Lindy said, leaning forward so I could see. He quick slipped a gigantic hook under its top fin. The fish flinched and squirmed, but Lindy said, "Can still swim this way." He dipped it in the water. "See?"

I nodded, and Lindy lifted the shiner back into the air and cast out, not very far. On the other side of the boat, Krankill did the same. Allen had me pass back his rod, and I took my own, looking at the tiny snelled Eagle Claw hook tied to the end of the line. I didn't have to open my tackle box to know I didn't have anything close to the size of hook I needed.

Lindy bumped my shoulder, holding out a hook.

"Thanks," I whispered.

"Tie that on all right?" he asked.

My face burned. "Yes."

"Usually we use wire leaders," Krankill said, "but brain-case Lindy left his box at home."

"We'll probably end up trolling," Allen said. "But for now, with all of us, we'll just sit here, see if anything happens. This is a pretty good spot."

I finished hooking my shiner. Looking away from its big round eye, I glanced around the lake. We were in the middle of nowhere, I thought, one spot out here the same as any other. But I cast out and let my line go a ways before setting my bail, showing them they didn't have to take care of me.

We sat a long time, all silently watching our rod tips, until Krankill finally started singing "Here fishy, fishy, fishy," low and quiet.

"I can feel him," Krankill went on. "Man oh man he's close. And man oh man he's hungry!"

I smiled bigger, retesting my grip on my rod. I'd never fished with anyone else before, and I glanced back to see what Lindy was doing, what Allen was doing. They were smiling, too, staring out at the points their lines made knifing into the quiet water. "Shut up, Krank'," Allen muttered, still smiling.

Krankill was quiet a while before he whispered, "Oh, he's coming, all right!" He hummed the "Bum dum, bum dum" music from *Jaws*. He shivered, trembling the whole boat.

"Oh man and is he big. Big and mean and nasty and grumpy and . . ."

My rod nearly jerked out of my hands. I leaped off the cooler to catch it, to grab it tight, to strike back as hard as I could, the boat teetering around me, everybody going low to keep us from tipping over. "Man!" Krankill screamed. "He's . . ."

But it was already finished and everybody went quiet and I cranked in my limp line, my face as red as the gas can behind Allen's feet. My reel had never been louder.

I lifted the line quick, wanting to hide my empty hook, but it wasn't empty and Lindy said, "Let me see that," snagging what was left of my shiner before I could hide it.

"Whoa," he said, whistling. He handed the shiner back to Allen, who said, "Now those are teeth marks! Krankill was right. It was a monster."

Lindy stuck the shiner in front of my face. Only the front half was left. The fish was bitten off a half inch behind my hook. That close. The teeth marks began in front of the hook, scraping backward, digging deeper until they reached the cut.

"Nothing gonna catch a fish that size," Krankill whispered, looking over my shoulder at the shiner half. "That's not even a fish. That's a sea monster. Loch Ness material."

"None of us would've caught it either," Allen told me, but he went on to say how you got to let them take the bait, let them get the whole thing down, two, three bites, before you hit them. "You hit him plenty hard," he said. "Just a little quick. But everybody does, first few times. When they hit the bait like that, you can't help yourself."

But none of them would've caught it either, I thought, knowing it was a lie.

Lindy gave me the shiner and I sat looking at it in my lap, remembering the lightning jolt of that strike, my hands all of a sudden starting to shake, shake even when I grabbed my knees to make them stop. I glanced across the flat water toward shore, the green-black line of trees in the distance, and tried to remember how to breathe.

When I could, I hooked up another shiner, and we sat in the boat, the four of us, for a long time, watching our lines, the three of them talking eventually, when nothing happened, about high school and fishing, and even girls a little. I listened this time, not missing anything, wishing I could do this with them every weekend, every single time they came out.

After an hour or two we started trolling, but we had too many lines and I reeled mine in, saying it was fair, I already almost had one. For less than one second, anyway.

Allen said, "No, I'll just steer the boat," but my line was already in by then, and he told me to have it my way.

Then, as we putted around the lake, slower than walking now, he started talking about northerns and walleyes, how anybody could fish for them, but the real fishing was for muskies. It didn't matter, he said, that you only hooked into one once, maybe twice a year. "Because," Krankill added, "man oh man when you do . . ." He just shook his head and whistled, knowing the words would never be invented.

And now I believed them, more than I ever had sitting in our living room, listening to Allen, watching him strain to hear Alice upstairs, wondering how long she was going to make him sit here talking to this kid.

Allen didn't point us back to the dock till it was almost evening, and then it was hard to pick out the shape there on the end of the planks. "I'll be dipped. . . ." Krankill started, and Lindy finished, saying, "Looks like Towers."

When we got close enough to see, I wanted to say, "It is! It is Towers!" like Tweety-bird. My imitation killed my friends. But I kept quiet.

"Couldn't find a ride," Allen said, sounding like he'd spit.

"Aw," Krankill said, "Towers isn't all bad."

As we pulled close Towers stood up. He was smoking a little cigar he'd found somewhere, and in one hand he held a bag of beer bottles, the long, brown neck of one tilting out. In the other he held up a stringer full of good-sized perch. "How'd you guys do?" he asked, as if he'd planned on perch fishing all along.

"Frank tied into one," Krankill answered.

"But it was too much for his line," Allen said.

Lindy threw Towers a rope and pretty quick we were all out of the boat, all back in the car, Towers's stringer in the trunk, his cigar stubbed into the gravel because Allen wouldn't let him stink up his car with it. The beer was in with us, yeasty and awful smelling as we drove and it got dark. Towers even offered me one, and I thought of Kranky saying "Towers isn't all bad."

I whispered, "No thanks."

At home they dropped me off without pulling into the driveway. Towers fed my rod out the half-open window, saying, "You'll get him next time, kid."

Allen came around to unlock the trunk so I could get my tackle box and my worms. "Sure you don't want to trade those for a Milky Way?" he said.

I shook my head. I'd been trying to rehearse a line since we'd climbed out of the boat, something to show him how great it'd been, how much I wanted to go again. But I only said, "Thanks for taking me."

"Sure thing," Allen said. "Anytime." He glanced toward the house. My dad was standing on the porch looking at us.

"Tell Alice I'd come in, but . . ."

"I know what you mean," I said, and he grinned, sitting back down behind the wheel. When he peeled out, my dad just shook his head, turning back inside.

It was Alice who met me at the door, not Dad. "How was it?" she asked right away, looking like she might need to pee.

"Fine," I answered. She had my way blocked.

"What did you talk about?"

"Nothing."

"Franky! What did *they* talk about?"

"Nothing."

She gave me a look and I said, "Just fishing, Alice."

She kept up the look. "They didn't say *anything?*"

"I almost got one, Alice!" I blurted, feeling again the thunder of that instant. "It was the biggest fish I've ever felt! It left *teeth* marks on my shiner!"

"But they must've said something. About me and Allen?"

I shook my head, surrounded by all the things they'd said and hadn't said, all the things I could never tell. "It was the biggest thing I've ever done, Alice."

She blew out her cheeks in frustration, blurting, "Fish!" and whirling inside.

I stayed alone on the porch a minute longer, holding onto my fishing rod and tackle box, looking down the line of glowing streetlights running away from our house. When I went in at last, Alice was only just inside the door, still waiting for me. Though we didn't know yet, this was only days before she and Allen took off together, my dad swearing he'd track them down.

"I can go with him anytime, Alice," I told her. "He said so."

For the Kid's Sake

So Rayney brings his kid this time, the three of us busting through brush that'd stop a Panzer. Since he has the kid with him, I let Rayney break trail. I don't know kids from kabobs; don't know what they can handle, what they can't, why this one's here at all. Rayney and I've been fishing together since grade school. Never brought anyone else with him before.

Watching his kid's back—ducking, weaving, even, I'll give it to him, *bulling* through the tangle—I guess he's ten or eleven, and I can't help wondering why Rayney never brought him before. How he ever got away with it.

We carry our rods cased, using them like shields now and then, and pretty soon I get a little grin out of it: Rayney smarter than I ever gave him credit for. I picture the kid—what the hell did he say his name was?—whining and pestering, *Take me fishing, Dad! I want to go!* Rayney finally giving in, only to take him to this hell on earth, a place Rayney and

I once blundered into and gave up on before ever reaching the ponds Rayney claimed to have spotted on his topos. Lashed across the face with a rose stem as thick around as my leg, I muffler a few choice lines—for the kid's sake—and marvel at the genius Rayney's kept under a bushel all the time I've known him. If the kid ever asks to go with us again, it won't be in this millennium.

I catch another something across the back of the hand, not remembering to keep in the swearing. I'm bleeding like I got knifed, and I turn to aim a kick at a buffaloberry the size of a sequoia, thorns like jousting lances. Up ahead Rayney yells, "Watch those thorns," and I hear the kid give a little chuckle.

Hilarious.

We still haven't spotted water, leastways I haven't at the back of the train, when the kid about vanishes, dropping into some hole. Up ahead Rayney's slashing at some stickery vine, wielding his old aluminum rod case like a machete, making way too much racket to ever hear his kid drop off the face of the earth.

I come up and the kid's struggling away, not calling after Rayney, not asking for help at all. I say, "How's it going?"

He spins his head around like he forgot I was there behind him. He's up to his waist in this hole.

"There's water in here," he says. "We must be getting close."

I glance around the thicket we're trapped in. "Sure hope so, anyway," I say.

The kid never stops grabbing at branches, half of them covered with barbs and cat-claws, pulling for all he's worth.

"Want a hand?" I ask.

"I'll get it," he says.

"Looks tight."

He just keeps pulling. He's not making an inch.

"That water cold?" I'm picturing his old high-tops, just like Rayney's fishing shoes. His blue jeans like mine.

"Pretty," he answers.

"Well then, maybe if there really are any ponds out here, there'll be trout in them."

"Hope so," he says. His hands are starting to look a little hamburgery.

Finally I can't stand it, and I reach down and shuck him out by the armpits. Makes a pop coming out, like a cork. "Could've been in there the duration," I say.

"Thanks," he answers. "But I was getting it."

I'm looking down the hole, then at his waist. Rayney'd say, "Like a thumb in an asshole," that tight, but I hold my tongue for the kid's sake.

Instead I say, "That's an old beaver hole. We got to be getting close."

He nods, and just then we hear Rayney yell, "Fish on!"

Sure, I think, while I'm hauling your kid out of the drink, saving his life. Rayney's never been one to share a fishing hole. Me neither, really, least not fishing with Rayney.

"Come on," I tell the kid. "Follow me." I veer away from Rayney's call, knowing he'll have the best casting spot staked out, that he won't budge for us.

After crashing along, eyes closed half the time to keep the bushes from augering them out, I step right into water. Hitting the mud, I go down, up to my waist myself, in the pond this time, not just some beaver sinkhole. Only a miracle keeps me from sliding under completely.

The water biting into my privates shocks a shout out of me, something that should've been *Sockpucker!* for the kid's sake, but wasn't.

I dart a look behind me to catch his shocked grin, but he's not there. In front of me, in the water, the silt billows out in mushroom clouds, littler tracers out front, tiny spurts of mud from the panicked dash of trout. Brookies probably, and if our way in is the only way (not a given, with Rayney navigating), brookies that have never seen a fly or a fly line in their lives.

From my fish-eye view, I see the whole swampy clearing, the brush finally laid low by the flooding of what must be a chain of a hundred beaver dams. If a guy walked out on the dams, away from the edges, watched out for the drowned snags of old aspen, there'd be room for a backcast, acres of untouched pond water to work.

I chili my hands clawing my way out of the pond, same way the kid did getting out of his hole. Where is he?

I look around quick, nothing but gray branches, dead leaves. Everything quiet. "Rayney!" I shout, the noise ugly and way too loud in the stillness of the tangle.

Closer than I expect I hear him answer, "For Pete's sake, what are you shouting about?"

"I lost your kid."

"What?"

"Your kid. Remember? He came with us."

"He's right here," Rayney says.

Just then the kid yells, "Fish on!"

Rayney asks, "You getting into any over there?"

"Tons," I answer, finally standing back on the bank, water pouring off my pants, squelching in my shoes. I start out on the first dam, this pond shot.

Water gushers around my shoes at each step on the old dam, but, since I've already been swimming, no harm done. If the sun ever burns the clouds off, my shiver will be gone quick. Glancing back at another call of "Fish on!" I see one rod tip held high, a tiny arc in it; the other, right beside it, just laying down a loop. Then there's another shout. "Fish on!"

I mutter more stuff the kid shouldn't hear.

At last, after slipping and stumbling across a string of little auxiliary dams, I'm crouched on the backside of the Grand Coulee of beaver dams, one that could crank out kilowatts, a big black lake of a pond untouched in front of me. I uncase and set up, listening to Rayney's and his kid's constant calls of "Fish on!"

Remembering the clouds of muck kicked up by the fleeing trout, I tie on a Prince Nymph, figuring the brookies might be too skittish for a dry. But when I finally get my first cast out, the fish fight over it as soon as it touches water. Could've been a cigarette butt. I keep my *Fish on!* to myself.

Though I catch glimpses of some burly old bastards, the ones beating each other up over my fly are standard beaver-pond material: six-, eight-, nine-inchers. Even so, their jaws are black and hooked, the colors flaming along their flanks. I change flies to something monstrous, a Woolly Worm the size of my thumb, but that only makes the fighting more frantic as the little trout struggle to stretch their gums around it.

While I'm working the dinks to death, I catch glimpses of Rayney and his kid migrating around the maze of dams and pools. "What the hell is that kid's name?" I ask myself out loud. I see he's got a stringer of fish dangling from a belt loop as he and his dad sneak along.

"You catching anything real?" I shout. "Or just these dinks?"

"Monsters all," Rayney shouts back, and again I hear his kid's giggle.

Of course I yuck it up pretty hard myself—drop-dead humor like that—but it's right while I'm thinking maybe there isn't anything hid under Rayney's bushel after all that one of the big battleship brookies finally shakes itself awake long enough to twitch a fin over and inhale my Woolly Worm.

I'm a hair late on the uptake—see the worm come spitting back out of that gaping black maw just as I'm hauling back to clear the slack and set the hook. So I set it even harder, as if that'll put the hook back where it belongs.

Well, the usual happens. With no seething slab of trout flesh there to stop it, all that line—the glob of yarn and feather and sharpened steel on the end—comes sailing back at me like a tangled hurl of soggy spaghetti. Same feeling as swinging through a fastball you're already planning on watching chunk into the cheap seats, or expecting one more step at the bottom of the stairs; that same uncomfortable, socket-rocking surprise.

I duck, squeezing my eyes shut, and lash the rod back down, hoping to get things reversed in time. Turns out that only powers things up, though, and the hook sets itself in my eyebrow, me already wondering, *Did I smash that barb flat or not?*

Turns out not.

I bite the line through, then sit on the dam, the water rushing past just below my belt. There's a little blood trickling into my eye, and I can feel the barb on the wrong side of my skin; gone through and back out. Same time I wonder if there's some way I cannot let Rayney find out about this, I wonder if he's carrying a needle-nose with a wire clipper somewhere in that junkman's fishing vest of his.

I'm voting on living with the hook rather than letting Rayney run loose with it, hoping my eyebrow's big enough and dark enough to hide the pound or so of Woolly Worm dangling from it, when Rayney shouts, "Hey, Monk! There's an island here. What say we build a fire and grill up some of the kid's fish for lunch?"

"'The kid,'" I murmur. He couldn't've actually named him The Kid. Why doesn't he just say his name once?

The walk over to their island isn't exactly recreation. They have to shout to me for a while, before I finally see the one aspen that's survived the flood on the high ground. When I get there, I just wade across the last pond rather than working around to the far side for the dam. Doesn't get me any wetter, really. It's good to see there's already smoke pillaring up from beneath the fluttery yellow leaves of the one live tree.

The sun never did get to work on the clouds and I hunker over the little flames, keeping my face and hat low, pushing in the entire supply of wood they'd gathered. "Colder than you'd guess out here," I mumble, thinking of all the "colder thans" Rayney'd be running off: than the balls of a brass monkey, a witch's tit, a cupful of crushed ice in a whore's ———. He's got a million of them.

But nobody, I notice, is saying anything. Or doing anything at all. Lifting my eyes without lifting my head, I peer around the shadow of the Woolly Worm, glance at their feet, see them pointing my way.

"Go for a swim?" Rayney finally asks.

"Just slipped some," I answer. "Getting to the big ones."

Rayney hums an answer. "I was wondering what hit that Woolly Worm of mine so hard. Busted me clean off."

The kid, of course, can't think of anything funnier he's ever heard in his life. I'm thinking, *Should I carry out the bodies, or bury them here?*

"Got any more wood?" I ask.

"We're roasting a few trout, Monk. Not a pig."

"I've got a chill going," I say.

Still without lifting my head, I listen to them spread out, picking up sticks. They may live through to sunset after all.

Stoking the flames up to bonfire proportions, we all stand there a while, backing up as the fire really takes hold. Finally I hear the clinking and clanking of Rayney rummaging through his vest. Pretty soon he holds a hook-nosed forceps underneath my face. "All I got," he says. "Could've sworn I had a few pliers in here."

"What good are forceps?" I ask.

"Smash down the barb," he says. "Back it out."

"Be better cutting it off."

"You're the expert," he says, "no doubt about that. But how are we going to cut the hook?"

Finally I'm sitting down, head back for all their fun, and Rayney's working on the barb. This isn't maybe half as fun as it sounds, but for once the kid is not smothering himself choking back the hee-haws. Least not till Rayney says, "What do you say, Bry, catch and release? Or should we just brain this old lunker and gut him out?"

Brian! That's his name.

"Just get on with it," I start to say, but before I get it all out Rayney gives this twisting yank and I gasp out something awful as my sphincter clamps shut and my gonads hit the back of my throat along with my heart and lungs. By the time I can open my eyes and clear away the tears, Rayney's dangling my Woolly Worm before me.

"That'll teach you to go barbless," he says.

I keep staring at the fly, not quite believing my eyebrow isn't twisting from the hook. I feel for it on my head, saying, "For ——— sake, where's my eyebrow?"

"Hey," Rayney says, sounding serious for maybe one of two times in his life. "Watch the mouth."

"Me?" I gasp, my wind still not quite back from his string-around-the-doorknob style of hook removal. Rayney could scorch the paint off a troopship with the way he talks most every day. I just gape at him. "Me?" I say again.

"There's a kid here," Rayney reminds me.

"No shit," I answer. "And if it weren't for me he'd still be stuck in a hole, some beaver gnawing at his knees."

"What?" Rayney asks.

"I was almost out," the kid whispers.

"So don't go talking to me about my language, Mister No-Sentence-Complete-without-the-F-Word!"

"What?" Rayney asks.

"What?" the kid asks.

"You rake yourself through three miles of barbed-wire brush," I say, "drop your ass into an ice-cold beaver pond, then hang your eyebrow off a number two Woolly Worm and see how lily white your tongue gets!" I got to admit, in the heat, I spice that up with a few expletives.

"I did all that, too, Monk. Except for your Woolly Worm problem. You know I'll never match your casting abilities."

"No shit," I say.

"But I'm serious about the mouth. Brian doesn't need that."

"It's not like I haven't heard it before, Dad," the kid says.

"See?" I answer.

"Well he doesn't need hearing it again. Not from me. Not from my friends."

"Friends?" I say. "Like what, your social circle just keeps expanding?" I give a snort. "I'm the only friend you ever had." My eyebrow's laying out more blood and I keep my hand pressed to it, squinting all one-eyed at Rayney, wondering what his surgery's cost me in the way of cosmetic appeal. He's been married forever, but I still have to rely on my looks.

"Just clean it up, Monk. That's all I'm asking."

"'Colder than a cupful of crushed ice in a whore's . . .'" I start to quote, but Rayney roars, "Enough!"

Really, I'm glad he stopped me, for the kid's sake. But I say, "Well, you invented that one. You got to admit that."

The kid, I can see, even one-eyed, is all ears, just gawping at his dad.

Rayney holds up his hands. "I know. Nothing to be proud of. But Monk, I haven't been that way since Brian was born."

I snort again. "My ass," I start to say, but slowly I start thinking maybe he's right, that maybe that'd all been in high school, before Rayney got himself married up so young, when decent people were just beginning to think about all those oats they were going to sow.

The kid drops out. He takes to worrying the fire with a big stick, not just roasting it and listening but working the fire, bunching up the sticks, dragging out coals, trying to pretend he's not here. Or that we're not.

And then, like it wasn't poking me there in the nose all day, it comes to me. The kid can fish. He can cast. He can make a fire.

I stare at him with my eye. There's one muck-black toe leaking out of his old high-tops. His jeans are dotted with fish blood. There's a leather string leading into his pocket that I know ends on a Swiss Army knife, just like Rayney always has. He's even wearing a little fishing vest, which is torn and restitched, the material sun faded where it isn't wet and muddy.

Good God, I think, the kid was never the one getting left behind. For the second time that day, I think that maybe Rayney has some light hiding beneath his bushel after all. Believe me, this is not something that has ever happened before.

I take a peek up at him. I just thought we both got busy working. I just thought he had a list of Honey-dos a mile long. I just thought he got trapped at home with a squalling kid, that otherwise we'd still be fishing as much as we used to.

I stand up, wiping the blood off my hand onto my soggy pants. The kid, I see, has pulled this little wisp of a grill out of his vest, unfolded it, and staked it out over the coals. All by himself he's stretching the little brookies onto it, watching them curl away from the heat.

Maybe he feels me staring at him. He turns my way and grins a little. "You like them this way?" he asks.

I almost say, *Hell, yes! I'm the guy that taught your dad how to cook them that way, without messing them up with all his goddamn marinades and shit!* But instead I simply nod and say, "They taste good, don't they, Brian? Just smoky and hot and clean."

He nods, pokes at a trout, flattening it back onto the grill. "I release most of them," he assures me, suddenly realizing he doesn't know where I stand on any of the big issues. "But sometimes . . ." He lets it fade.

I'm a stranger, after all, a foul-mouthed old friend of his dad's. There's no telling how much I'll understand.

Mighty Mouse and Blue Cheese from the Moon

I wasted the whole drive in to see her. It's a three-hour trip, through the mountains at first, along the river, where I try to pick out fishing holes as I drive. Then the road passes the first swampy, beaver-clotted pools of the river and climbs along a single, minuscule feeder creek to the divide. After that it's hard to remember the timber and the dark curves of the canyons because you're into the high plains. They roll wildly, but smoothly, the rough edges burred off by the wind, and they go on forever. But I missed it all with my daydreaming. I was too anxious to see her and to be alone with her on the river.

Like a fool, the first thing I asked was if she was ready to go. We stood there in the living room, holding each other. We were laughing about something, I can't remember what, when I asked. She didn't answer right away so I told her how the night would be. "There's a storm billowing up in the south," I said, letting her go to swing my arms to show the size of the clouds. "But it's clear all around them."

I was trying to get her excited, but as she let me go it seemed that she might have had other plans for the evening.

"We'll float right on the edge of it, with the sky going all purply, the first flecks of stars coming out, the blackness in the thunderheads, maybe the temperature dumping twenty degrees or so."

She said, "That'd be nice," and she smiled. She wasn't excited about having to drive fifty miles by herself just to run the shuttle, but she smiled about that, too, saying I was a hopeless romantic to want to drive all the way to Great Falls to see her through my rearview mirror for fifty miles.

She got her stuff together and we drove out, bumper to bumper on the pretty much deserted interstate. I bucked around with the canoe catching the wind and she waved whenever she caught me watching her in the mirror. I pointed out a coyote, then a group of pelicans that wheeled over the river by Cascade, flashing white when their backs caught the sun then disappearing when they turned away. Like a flying wing of signal mirrors. When I looked to see if she'd seen them she had both hands clasped above her head waving them from side to side in an old-time boxer's victory salute. Like Mighty Mouse used to do.

We left her truck at Craig then drove together the last five miles, babbling like high school dates. It'd been a long time since then, but after finally getting married we'd only gone a month before my "little" out-of-town job came up. That was six months ago and now I was only seeing her every other weekend. So we went on and on for the five minutes, talking of nothing in particular.

We got the canoe in and loaded and Mary zipped herself into a life vest—she doesn't fish but she's not much for swimming, either. The storm had come up a lot faster than I expected and she pointed at the thunderheads, her hair pulling around to the wind, and rolled her eyes and stepped into the bow. We'd formed the habit, years ago, when she was just learning to canoe, of my always taking the stern, where you steer from, you know. Now, though she could pilot as well as I could, she did it from the front. I fished from the stern. Didn't make much sense, but that's how we did things.

"So where's dinner?" she said, paddling, without turning around, before I'd even set up a rod. It was an old joke—we hardly ever keep fish—and I laughed the way you do at old jokes when they remind you of all the other times you've heard them.

I'm not up on fishing the way some people are. I mean, I found my fly rods on the bottom of this very stretch of river. I've floated all my life, and swum, and done some fishing, too, but I don't know about barometric pressure, or pH, or all that other high-tech fishing mumbo-jumbo. Anyway, there was nothing rising, so I set up the rod with the sinking line and tied on a big, black, weighted nymph. I think it was a Hellgramite but wouldn't want to have to bet on that. I found my fly box, too, but not on the Missouri.

A rip of thunder let go, closer than I'd have guessed, and it startled a gasp out of me. Mary really laughed at that, waving her paddle above her head.

I turned to shoot the clouds a look and you wouldn't've believed how close they were. And coming on like nobody's business. Mary caught me at that, too. "We're going to get schmeered," she said. "I love it when you take me on dates."

We were a couple of miles into the float, just before the wind really went crazy, carrying rain with it, when I finally hooked into something besides all those false little tugs the bottom gives out.

I could feel the fish was small, but hooked solid, so I was puffing and pulling, grunting things like "Water on the reel!" whenever the fish would make a run to click out a few feet of line.

It even broke the surface once—not jumped really, broached was more like it—and I hollered, "Tie me in!" Then, as I was crying "Nantucket sleigh ride!" she caught a good look at the fish. It was a whitefish, which was what I was beginning to suspect, and she chanted "Snout-trout, snout-trout" until the rain let loose.

There was the usual scramble for rain gear that we always put off too long. For some reason she was laughing so hard you couldn't tell if she was squeezing out tears or if it was just the rain.

I got pretty wet before getting the gear on because I had to unhook the whitefish. But when that rain let go, it let go. Usually the wind goes berserk before one of these storms gets on top of you, then dies out when the rain takes over. But this one just kept howling. I ruddered with my paddle and we were like a speedboat, driving downstream before the wind.

We were both laughing then. The lightning was blasting the cliffs, the thunder right with it, shaking your insides like it does so close. It was like being in our own hurricane and it was something to feel. It had gone dark and Mary turned to me. She'd pulled her hood back and her hair was stringy and wild with the rain. She was grinning, her teeth so white it was scary. We were putting up a bow wave by then.

We started to pass rafts that'd pulled over, the occupants huddled underneath, and she went into her Mighty Mouse thing again, even screaming with the wind. The landlocked boaters waved back, though she must've looked like a river banshee.

We went all the way into Craig like that. She was so worked up I knew there was something alive in there that she was dying to get out. She gets so excited about things. Like this storm. It couldn't have been better if I'd planned it for her. And she's tough, you know. Wind and rain wouldn't touch her. But she has trouble saying things, like tough guys usually do. That's where the whole Mighty Mouse thing came from. She'd get so fired up her tongue wouldn't work and she'd have to flash that grin and wave her arms around like a cartoon character.

We weren't quite so ecstatic tying down the canoe. Rain gear never works all the way and those wet spots were pretty cold once we started moving around. But we stripped it off soon enough and, with the windows fogging up, decided to leave my truck at Wolf Creek so we could drive back to the Falls together. She even sat next to me, like a cowboy's girl, and I put my arm around her, which is not the way we usually drive. I pointed out that with my truck at Wolf Creek we'd be able to float again in the morning without having to drive apart. She said that'd be great and, sopping wet though she was, I think she would've agreed to anything. Her head was pressed into my shoulder and I could feel the water soak into my shirt.

It was still dark when I woke the next morning and Mary's head was still on my shoulder. She was breathing real slow and quiet and it was good just to hold her like that. I knew if we left soon we'd get dawn on the Missouri, and by the reddish light through the window I knew that would be a bad thing to miss. Pretty soon I wanted to get up and get a lunch together and a thermos so all she'd have to do was get dressed—about as close as we get to breakfast in bed. But she sleeps like a cat and I knew I didn't have a chance of sneaking out. She likes lying in in the morning, half awake, whispering and dozing. She says it's when she does her best thinking. Me too, I guess, but if I'm going to have something as rare as an idea I don't want to be in bed when it happens. Lying in bed too long makes my back hurt anyway.

So I tried to sneak out and it didn't work. I brought her a cup of coffee a few minutes later and told her that it was clear out and how the river would be this early with the fog after the rain and how it would smell. She just lay there and said she wanted to stay in and talk this morning since I was here and we could do it.

"Nobody else floats this early," I told her. "We'll have the river to ourselves and it'll be brand new after the storm."

She sniffed at the coffee. "I just wanted to lie here with you and talk. There's things we need to talk about." She touched my hand. "You and me, me and you."

I felt the morning slipping away, the fog replaced by fishermen. I bounced on the bed a little and called her a lazy bones, or something like that, and told her there were no rules against talking on the river. She glared at me a second then said, "Oh, goddamn it," and threw the covers back and stalked into the bathroom and closed the door. I could hear her getting dressed.

I was pretty surprised and I called through the door that we could stay in bed, it didn't matter. She didn't answer and I stood there, wiggling my toes in my wading boots. When she came out she was dressed and she said, "Let's go."

I said again, "Let's stay," but she gave me a look, took her coffee cup, and headed down the back stairs for the truck.

I followed down, not too worried. It was no good seeing her like this, but everybody wakes up like that once in a while. With the river and a little coffee she'd be Mighty Mouse again before I knew it.

It was a stony ride down, though, and when she didn't even reach for the thermos I was starting to remember what a nice drive it was last night, with her in another truck. I cracked the thermos myself, driving with my knee, and that smell filled the cab. She reached out her cup and even tried to smile. "Thanks," she said. She never stays mad for long.

She held her cup a long time, looking out over the dawn, saw it reflecting back off Square Butte. The river was nothing but a ribbon of fog in the bottom. Then she sipped her coffee and winced.

"Too hot?" I asked, like there was something I could do about it.

"This is decaf," she said. "It's not what I needed this morning." She looked like her whole world had just caved in.

"Decaf?" I said, sounding pretty slow. I'd only made what was there.

"I can still have one cup of decent coffee in the morning," she said, sounding mean and pissy at once.

"Okay," I said. I poured my own cup. I'd never had decaf and I was wondering what it would taste like. It'd beat conversation this morning.

She drank two cups before we got there, so it couldn't have been too terrible. The only other thing she did was put on another sweatshirt. It wasn't cold, but it would be on the water. I figured she was looking at that web of mist, feeling its chill.

We ran the little shuttle to get a truck at the takeout and then drove to the put-in again—without a word being spoken. The fog was breaking some but the sun wasn't over the hills yet. That would take a few hours. And there wasn't another car or truck at either access. We had it to ourselves.

When the canoe was loaded we stood next to the river a moment. It was quiet, like pin-dropping quiet, but it really wasn't with the water rustling along and a little breeze through the alder and roses. Mist hung head high, so we could see across the steamy river but the whole world was only as tall as we were, like we could bump our heads on it. It was safe somehow and it had that kind of loneliness that you wouldn't mind having all the time. I put my arm around Mary and forgot to be surprised when she returned the hug.

"Are we off?" I whispered, and she nodded and climbed into her bow seat. I pointed her into the slow current and pushed, the river splashing my boots as I stepped into the canoe.

I gave a few shots with my paddle then gave control over to Mary and picked up the same rod I'd used the day before. I'd set it up this time, so I could at least get a cast in before she asked where breakfast was.

Like I said, I'm no expert fisherman, and that heavy fly was throwing me off and Mary was just sitting there letting the boat drift sideways. I was still getting line out when I saw her hand go up and she said my name and "Stop." I knew right away I'd caught her, though I'd never done anything like that before. It made me feel sick.

I let the rod down and looped the line out of the water so it wouldn't drag and asked, "Where?"

I was already shuffling along to her seat and saw her holding onto the fly, which was in her neck, a little above her collar. The canoe rocked a little, nothing even close to spectacular, and she said, "Go to shore."

"I don't think it's anything," I said. "I can see the barb."

"Go to shore!" she said, practically spitting. I sat down where I was and paddled from there.

125

We crunched into the little pebbles on the opposite bank and I splashed out and pulled us up, saying I was sorry one more time.

She didn't get out and she wouldn't look at me when I crouched beside her. I waited a little; the hook was on the far side, so I couldn't do anything. "Mary," I whispered, and she sat quietly, turned toward the shrouded river. Finally I walked around the canoe and through the tiny riffle to her and squatted again. She lifted her face for me to see the hook and I couldn't have been more shocked if Mighty Mouse had gotten a bite of that blue cheese from the moon and crashed into the center of the Missouri. Tears were coursing down her cheeks, big, rolling drops, one after the other. I stared at them for a second. I'd never seen them there. Then I reached forward to hug her and ask her what in the world was wrong. It wasn't the hook—you could gaff Mary without her giving you the satisfaction of a single flinch.

She leaned into the hug, not sniffing or shuddering— nothing but those tears. Pretty soon she sighed. "Take out the hook."

I let her go some, and asked her what was wrong. She shook her head and wiped at the tears, and I knew I'd never get it from her now. I looked at the hook and would've laughed any other time. The point was just pressed in. It was surprising it'd stayed in all this time. I moved it backward and it fell out. "There," I said, as if I'd solved all our worldly problems.

I sat in the water, next to her in the boat, wishing she'd just out and tell me about it. I knew I might as well wait for the rainbows to start leaping into the boat, and when she said I should probably try a fly I knew how to cast I moved back and pushed us out into the river.

She didn't even reach for her paddle, and I knew the fishing was done anyway. So I paddled slowly, trying to make no sound, and I watched the little whirlpools flank my paddle blade as it moved through the clear water. We glided with the main flow, wisps of fog giving way before us and closing back in behind us.

"It seemed like it must be when you're still in your womb, back there," she started saying all at once. "Closed in by water, everything quiet, and everything before you hidden by fog. Everything you might be. Every, every, everything."

She hadn't turned around or moved a muscle. Then she shivered and held herself a little closer as I stared at her back. "What?" I whispered. It was the only thing I could think to say and I was ashamed for sounding so slow.

She shook her head and a little snort of wind pushed the bow to the side and I swept the paddle to keep us on course. Neither one of us said anything for a long time, though I watched her sitting alone, going down the river before me.

The sun finally reached over the hills and touched us on that long straightaway. It's the first place that gets the sun and that we were there was just luck. The last of the mist was gone in seconds, and watching it go I thought this is the prettiest place in the world right now and then Mary said she loved me.

That's not so rare that it'd knock me out of the boat, but it wasn't what I was expecting right then. To tell the truth, I was looking then at the sun and the long hills, yellowed for an instant, and the shine off the cliffs before us. It was one of those times you're afraid will be too fast to see it all, and I'd sort of forgotten Mary was there. Not forgotten, but you know what I mean. It surprised me is all, and I practically said "What?" again. For crying out loud.

I felt lost in a way. It wasn't one of those times you just say, "Oh yeah, me too, Mar'." It was a bad time for her on a day that couldn't have been better if you'd made it yourself, and she was reaching out for something, to me. And through it all I tried to watch the sun coming up and how it changed everything around me, clearing the fog and giving that clear, soft light to old, almost worn-out things, and I felt guilty about trying to shut out everything else long enough to watch.

I was trying to figure a way to ask the question that would unlock what was inside her when the fish started to rise. It was more like the river was rising. First a few small, slurping swirls, then everywhere, shore to shore. Mary asked what was happening and I thought that's what I should have asked. But I only answered, "They're feeding."

"Catch them," she said, simply enough.

I saw the tiny, black, white-winged bugs and I knew they were tricos—don't ask me how, it's just one of maybe two bugs I do know. That and caddis, which all look like tent-wings to me.

I picked up my dry rod and looked in my box and had a whole row of Tricos, eighteens and twenties. That might happen to you all the time, but usually when I do know what's happening I don't have anything to match it.

I tied on the smallest and looked at the river. There seemed no point in casting anywhere in particular. Like flock-shooting a thick covey, it seemed you couldn't miss. But I do know how well that works, so I picked a rise and dropped the fly a ways in front of it and let it drift. It went right over and on so I left it to float. It was almost scary, like you didn't know what was under there or what had started them going like that, how they all knew to go at once. So I left the little fly on the water, too lost to pick it up and try again, because I wouldn't know what to do with it the next time either.

"Uh oh," she said, and I started to look at her, when, out of the corner of my eye, I saw the fly go. I wasn't quite thinking of it or Mary yet, so when I did hit, the line sailed back in limp curls, with the fly floating at the end of all that slack.

"Try it again," she whispered. She was up front, of course, and the way the boat and the fly were, she'd seen the trout coming up. That's why she'd said "Uh oh" before it even got there.

She was hunched a little and you could tell there was something in this she had to see. I cast again, down the length of the canoe, so it'd be right in front of her. I was flock-shooting now, I guess, but you do hit one now and then even doing that.

Sure enough, it'd only touched down when that little sucking swirl took it under and I hit back. The way they were all over, the rises I mean, and all such dainty slurps, I was wondering if we weren't into the whitefish hole of all time. But as soon as I hit, out he came, a big, big rainbow, dancing and shaking, then splashing and running cross-river, with me hardly doing anything right because I was still trying to watch him shaking in the first sun when he wasn't even there anymore.

Mary had her paddle out and was moving the canoe around, doing everything right to help me keep the fish. I don't know how she knew what to do, I wouldn't even have thought of moving the canoe. Big fish don't happen to me very often.

He kept running till I tightened up to what I thought must be too much. Then he broke out again and Mary whooped and I tried to gather slack as he ran back in on me, wondering why he even bothered to stay on.

At each jump, with him all silvery, not really rainbow looking yet because he was too fast for anything but flashes of silver to keep up with, he'd have his way. Not so much that he was making all the right moves but that I would freeze, so I could see him before he was gone. It never worked, of course, but I couldn't stop trying.

Even though I couldn't have done anything else to let him get off, pretty soon he tired down some and the jumps got weaker and the runs more easily turned and then he was beside the boat. I held him up front and Mary watched him finning calmly, head into the current, probably wondering what was going to happen to him next.

"Take him off," she said.

I eased him back and he made one last try, ratcheting out about ten feet and breaking out in a jump that had all that was left in him, and Mary jumped up in the front of the boat, giving the Mighty Mouse cheer to the fish, and I guessed to the sun and the river and maybe the whole world that wasn't us in that boat in that second.

She shook her clenched hands again and again, first over one shoulder then the other. I sat in the bottom where I'd dropped when she bounced up like that and watched her, forgetting all about the trout. But there he was, sitting beside the boat, ready to come out.

Mary sat down when I reached over the side and cradled a hand under the trout. She sat backward, facing me, and I held the trout, which was like a pet by then, not even quivering to the touch. The hook of that tiny, drowned fly was like the one in Mary that morning. All I did was pull back on the line and it drifted off his mouth without even a flinch.

Mary said, "Lift it up. Let me see it," and I did. He could've been the biggest trout I'd ever caught. I can never remember and Mary says I'm always saying that.

When I lowered him back to the water Mary said, "No. Kill it."

I looked at the trout, which was all rainbow now that he was still, at the rosy run down the line of his side, and the flares of red, and I did not want to kill him. I looked to Mary, because that's never something she says, even when she does want to eat one.

"Kill it," she said again, not looking at me but at where my hands held the fish in the water.

"But Mary," I started, knowing I didn't have anything to say after that. Nothing was that fish's fault. All I had to do was rub him a few times and let go, but I wasn't sure if I could do that to Mary and whatever was in her this morning.

I started to lift him out again, holding a little tighter since I knew care was no longer required. I was trying, even then, to see just one of his flashing jumps, the curve of the whip-spring body, but knew it was over and I'd never have the time.

Mary said, "Let him go," very softly, and I was afraid to look at her because I didn't know who I would find up there. I put the fish back in the water and stroked his sides until I felt him stir. I gave him a push then and he was gone and I smiled looking at where he had escaped.

I heard a tiny sob from the front of the boat, and Mary whispered that she was pregnant and that she was just afraid she was losing everything that had ever happened to her before and that she was sorry but she didn't know what she was doing and that she never knew pregnancy would be like this.

I stared for a moment longer at the trout that was gone and I thought I saw him in midleap and thought that I would always be able to. And when I looked up Mary was smiling and there were two more of her big, rolling tears, and she gave the weakest Mighty Mouser I've ever seen, but I could still see her waving wildly in the slanting sun, something whip-springy in her own way.

I'm not always slow, but I still wasn't sure I'd heard everything she said. Me and thinking are kind of like me and fishing, you know? I don't mean I found my brain on the bottom of the river, but I don't ever get so far into it I'm wondering about the pH or barometric pressure of everything I do or everything that happens to me. Mostly that's it, things happen to me. Like this. I don't go around thinking them up. I can't keep up with things the way they are. I've got to react to what happens, and I'm not the speediest reactor, so it was a moment or two before I stepped up and gave her a Mighty Mouse of my own. It was the only thing I could think to do.